Death for Gaia

Ecocide and the Righteous Assassins

Samuel Alexander and Peter Burdon

For Dash

DEATH FOR GAIA
Ecocide and the Righteous Assassins

Published by the Simplicity Institute, 2020
www.simplicityinstitute.org

Cover image by Andrew Doodson © 2020
Layout and typesetting by Sharon France (Looking Glass Press)
Typeset in Trajan and Stone Sans

ISBN: 978-0-6488405-0-3 (paperback)
ISBN: 978-0-9942828-9-7 (ebook)

PREFACE

We have always tried to write books full of ideas that are dangerous and unsettling. None, however, have felt quite as dangerous or unsettling as this one. Readers will quickly draw parallels between the virus described in this book (Hemlock-42) and the outbreak of COVID-19 (coronavirus) at the beginning of 2020. It is worth noting that our manuscript was complete and under review in July 2019, many months before the government in Wuhan, China, identified a new virus or the first death was reported. Any similarities between COVID-19 and Hemlock-42 are thus purely coincidental, and we offer this book with condolences to those who have lost loved ones to the pandemic.

The authors also wish to be explicit that we do not support the theory that COVID-19 was manufactured in a laboratory and deliberately released into the public. We recognise that the publication of this book comes at a very sensitive moment—we are writing these words in March 2020—so we will not be promoting it at this time, beyond our immediate networks. But we quietly release the text based on our belief in the importance of the issues it raises. We trust that it will be received in this spirit of unfiltered intellectual and ethical inquiry.

The authors would like to thank Mark Burch, Jacob Garrett, Ross Inness-McLeish, and Alex Reilly for their engagement and comments on earlier drafts of this book. The work was greatly improved by their generosity, intelligence, and their embodiment of a writing community. This book owes other intellectual debts, most notably to a law review article written by Lon Fuller in 1949: *The Case of the Speluncean Explorers*. As law students, we were both moved by Fuller's ability to usher readers through a set of judicial opinions each as plausible as the next. We have tried to recreate something of Fuller's style in this text and have been guided by his instigation to think for oneself and question comfortable assumptions.

Beyond Fuller's inspiration, this book has drawn on a rich heritage of legal, philosophical, ecological, and political thinking. Throughout the book a reader might notice that key traditions and thinkers are invoked, usually implicitly, to explore various perspectives, including prominent (and sometimes provocative) figures like Socrates, Aristotle, Immanuel Kant, Jeremy Bentham, Hannah Arendt, Judith Butler, Derrick Jensen, George Monbiot, Theo Simon, John Zerzan, and many others. For the most part we have avoided using direct quotes from thinkers so that readers can suspend reality and fully immerse themselves in the hypothetical conversation we have created.

Last but not least, we would like to acknowledge and express gratitude to the wonderful group of people who helped turn this manuscript into a book. Thanks to Andrew Doodson for the cover design; thanks to Sharon France for typesetting the book; and thanks to Antoinette Wilson for proofreading it. Although the following text is fundamentally a book of ideas not a novel, we're especially grateful to Antoinette for also helping us refine some of the literary aspects of the book's framing. The authors, of course, take full responsibility for the flaws that certainly remain.

CONTENTS

Ted Kaczynski, known to the FBI as the Unabomber, sent parcel bombs from his shack to those he deemed responsible for the promotion of the technological society he despises. Is it possible to read someone like Kaczynski and be convinced by the case he makes, even as you reject what he did with the knowledge?

Paul Kingsnorth, *Dark Ecology*

1. THE FINAL WARNING

In the year 2027, the Association of Concerned Earth Scientists (ACES) published a 'final warning to humanity'. Over one thousand pages long—and the most peer-reviewed document in human history—it detailed with forensic precision the catastrophic environmental impacts of human activity and urgently called for fundamental changes to what were described as civilisation's 'destructive tendencies'. The scientific report was accompanied by executive summaries, policy documents, guidance for activists, and an almost embarrassingly slick public relations campaign, copiously funded by anonymous philanthropists. For a short time, the 'final warning' was in the newspapers and a topic of cultural conversation.

Four months after publication, however, it had been forgotten, and the politics of willful blindness resumed. Radicalised by this ongoing global inaction and apathy, a secret faction developed within the board of ACES. These vigilantes were determined to make an impact on civilisation by taking things into their own hands, in order to contain what one of them described as the 'human plague'. Within a matter of months this underground collective of despairing scientists had developed a biological weapon they called 'Hemlock-42'. This virus, named after the poison used to execute Socrates, was designed with a single goal in mind: to eradicate most of humanity, as a means of preserving what remained of the biosphere and its dwindling diversity of species. Less than ten percent of the human population had a genetic immunity to the disease and those people were scattered randomly around the world.

The first two scientific warnings to humanity, published in the years 1992 and 2017, had gone unheeded, failing to change the trajectory of industrial civilisation. When the third warning also fell on deaf ears, the highly contagious Hemlock-42 was released, killing approximately seven-and-a-half-billion people within months. Best estimates place the surviving population at just under one billion people.

Thus industrial civilisation came to an abrupt and harrowing end.

A new age dawned in the chaotic aftermath. With the human population decimated by the virus and the systems of global capitalism shattered, Gaia was able to take pause from the onslaught of industrialism—just as the vigilantes had hoped. For the remaining wanderers of Earth it was surprising how quickly nature reclaimed her space in even the most 'civilised' of places. While plastics remained, the air and waters cleared of pollution, the forests slowly remerged in the forgotten fields of agriculture, and wildlife dared to walk or fly through the eerily quiet streets of central business districts. It wasn't long before the supermarket shelves were emptied by hungry survivors, suddenly aware of their dependency on dead modes of production and distribution, and in time the electricity and water grids stopped functioning. The Internet became a matter of lore and legend, such that children of the After World were never sure it had actually existed. To them it seemed quite implausible.

Suffering was everywhere, but so were beauty, peace, and regeneration. There is no short or easy means of describing the ways of living that emerged after the Great Die-Off. Suffice to say that the one-dimensionality of globalised, consumer culture disintegrated into fragments of local survivalism, adaptation, and frugal creativity. In the search for security, some banded together as marauders in the hope of reclaiming the false promises of affluence. But overall humanity fell into, or actively sought to establish, new and diverse forms of what was once called tribal community, making the best of a dead civilisation on a beautiful planet.

Some tribes hunted and gathered; others formed small farming communities; but most of what remained of humanity came to participate in various, hybrid forms of the salvage economy, reinhabiting empty buildings in the suburbs, inheriting 'abandoned' farms, bartering here and there with neighbouring communities, and basically making do with what they could find in the abundant treasures and waste streams of industrial civilisation. The cities of old had become as sparsely populated as the rural regions, and communication between bioregions was slow or non-existent. Fragments of news about far-away places sometimes arrived by way of sail or horse-and-carriage, and occasionally, in places, a car or truck would move slowly through the streets, powered by the last drops of ancient sunlight or fat scraped from the bottom of a deep-fryer. Everything was turned upside down and inside out, never to be the same.

Forty-six years after this momentous disruption, various tribes of one small corner of the After World have gathered, in this period of fragile but renewed stability, to discuss the justifiability of the acts that led to the Great Die-Off. Professor Durruk Senjen, the sole surviving activist who released Hemlock-42, has been called to defend his acts and face judgement. After living in exile for an indeterminate number of years, Senjen eventually became a wandering tradesman under cover of disguise, but several months ago he was recognised by two aging farmers as the man who created the virus. He was immediately detained and locked in a stone tower, where he has remained. As news of this slowly spread, thousands of people have travelled from far and wide to discuss what is to be done with him. Senjen has reluctantly agreed to explain himself, seeing no alternative, and attends the gathering of the tribes as a free man, albeit one fearing for his life.

The question under consideration: Was it right to deliberately destroy industrial civilisation, with all the human death and suffering this brought, for the sake of maintaining a healthy and thriving planet?

Or was it a heinous, arrogant, and unjustifiable crime for which the surviving perpetrator should be held accountable? Given that there are no longer any legal institutions or codes, these proceedings are not intended to be a 'trial' in the old sense. Instead, they were conceived of as explorations in truth, understanding, and the possibility of reconciliation, all the while knowing that many people would come with a hunger for retribution and punishment.

Zola Eblo, a respected elder of a distant community, has gained a reputation as a skilled healer and has earned the trust of her community through the patient hours she has spent nursing the unwell back to health or easing their transition into death and beyond. Because Zola stands at the veil between life and death she is also regarded as a spiritual guide who can be turned to in times of trouble.

When news of Senjen's detainment reached her community, Zola went quiet for several days. She withdrew from her community and sought solitude in a woodland on the outskirts of her village. There, in the midst of nature, she entered a meditative trance for three days and three nights, and when the wind blew from the East the townspeople could hear her singing faintly on the breeze. When Zola emerged, she was sombre, as though carrying a great weight on her shoulders. She sent a messenger to the community that was holding Senjen, offering to facilitate the discussion. Her offer was gratefully accepted.

The following discussion took place around a fire pit, in the ruins of what was once a great city, in the year 2073.

2. DEEP LISTENING

It is a warm, clear evening in late summer, in a region of the world now known as Bataluk. The sun sets over a dilapidated tennis stadium, once an open-aired venue for sporting and musical events but now only the home of weeds and wind. Hundreds of people begin to gather around a large bonfire at the centre of this makeshift amphitheatre, with most taking a seat on the ground in anticipation of the ceremony's commencement. As more people file in, they position themselves in a semi-circle on the tiered, concrete steps of the stadium, eyes facing toward the dancing flames that hold most of them in a meditative trance. Others talk quietly amongst themselves but soon fall silent. Despite the deteriorating state of the venue, there is a quiet dignity about the space that softens their tongues and eschews conversation or jocularity.

Most ethnicities and cultures of the After World seem to be represented in a vivid display of human diversity. Some are from regions where, it is rumoured, war abounds, but those gathered have agreed that intertribal disputes will be put to the side in recognition of the singular importance of this event. It is to be a gathering of peace and solidarity, of deep listening, albeit one burdened by the unhealed feelings of grief, anger, and loss that have brought the people together.

Nevertheless, children bring some lightness to the occasion by joyfully distributing fruit and nuts, and directing people to the barrels of drinking water, delighted at the interactive responsibility. Elders and community leaders have been asked to gather near the front to help guide and facilitate this unprecedented assembly of distant tribes.

When the last rays of light have almost disappeared behind the crumbling clock tower in the distance, an elderly woman moves to stand in front of the fire. All eyes turn to her and she begins to circle the stone fire pit, chanting to the heavens and the earth while breaking into a youthful and spirited dance. Her long grey dreadlocks are cast about in a poetic frenzy, and occasionally her eyes rise to meet the gaze of the attentive tribespeople. Many of those assembled break away from their tribal groups to join the elder in her dance. Boundaries are dissolved and the dancers morph into an indistinct community of graceful movement and expression.

The elder's song, which began as a complex and sublime melody without words, slowly evolves into a simple but entrancing chant, which soon is supported in chorus by the tribespeople:

> *'Blue Star, We are Thy Tears, The Guidance of Gaia, We Seek;*
> *Great Spirit, the Fire in our Eyes, Before Thee, We Speak.'*

A crescendo of percussion and harmonies builds to a climax, after which each cycle of the chant gradually becomes quieter and the collective dance becomes slower and lower. In time the peoples of the land sit down, at which point they are invited to reach out and clasp a hand of their nearest two neighbours. While most take up this invitation others are unfamiliar with such basic human contact and stare self-consciously into their lap. Heads are bowed and for an indeterminate moment the community revels in the unceasing eloquence of silence, ears touched only by the soothing crackle of the fire.

The elder begins to speak in a strong but compassionate voice. Her words resonate clearly around the stadium, reaching the multitude that has gathered without amplification.

The ceremony is underway.

We are one; we are many; we are alone, together, here and now, in sacred community.

We bow our heads in prayer and poetry; in gratitude and humility, to the divinity within and to the divinity beyond.

Let us listen to the Great Spirit; to the Poem of Creation; to the beat of one's own heart; to the life-force within, that flows seamlessly into the life-force beyond; through each other, and for each other.

Feel the touch of the dancing breeze that moves silently between us, the spirit that softly kisses your face as it kisses mine, under this infinite expanse, on this divine evening, connected by and through Gaia's embrace, at once fierce and all-loving.

Feel the warmth of your neighbours' hands; the roughness of their skin; a roughness made up of stories, just as we are all made up of stories, stories that have made our skin rough but left our inner beings tender and vulnerable; always tender and vulnerable.

Tonight, may our eyes adjust to the darkness within us and around us, as we practise Dadirri, deep listening, so that we come to see more clearly the path of our demise; so that we may one day rise, like a Phoenix, from the ashes of Empire, new creatures of the earth and sky.

We are one; we are many; we are alone, together, here and now, in sacred community.

We bow our heads in prayer and poetry, in gratitude and humility, to the divinity within and to the divinity beyond.

Three times let us pray:

> *Blue Star, We are Thy Tears, The Guidance of Gaia, We Seek;*
> *Great Spirit, the Fire in our Eyes, Before Thee, We Speak.*

My friends, I invite you now to open your eyes; to acknowledge each other as brothers and sisters, as children of Gaia, as matter awakening in the cosmos, in the beauty of our infinite diversity; to acknowledge the Earth and the Great Spirit, her creatures and creations, her mysteries and her music, her shadows and her song.

Together let us imagine pushing our fingers into the soil beneath us, in recognition of our most intimate connection and co-dependence. We are thankful for these great lands; for the mighty deserts and rainforests; for the flowing rivers and the hills; and for each of our fellow Earth creatures, glorious in their uniqueness and of value unto themselves. In grace and solidarity, we commit to live in humble service to the community of life.

Three times let us pray:

> *Blue Star, We are Thy Tears, The Guidance of Gaia, We Seek;*
> *Great Spirit, the Fire in our Eyes, Before Thee, We Speak.*

My friends, I am Zola Eblo. Beneath this Red Magnetic Moon I have been called to welcome one and all to this meeting of the tribes; at this time of Dadirri; this time of deep listening.

What a profound joy it is to see the children of Gaia gathered this evening in peace, our numbers fading into the dancing shadows. I salute thee! May we learn from this time of deliberate peace and remember that our concerns dissolve upon our mindful command, if only we show the courage to sit quietly, breathe slowly, and listen to the four winds. Trust thyself and each other, for the Great Spirit which guides us will keep us safe.

And yet my voice trembles. A joy though it is to be gathered here in sacred community, we have been brought together this evening to meditate on the darkness which lies in our history, and which inevitably shapes our constitution and gives colour and texture to the fabric of our existence. We gather here not to celebrate, alas, but to reflect on matters of violence, death, and demise; to seek a deeper understanding of the disruptive events which have shaped the centre and circumference of our lives on this far side of industrial civilisation's collapse.

I am speaking specifically, of course, of the Great Die-Off, through which most of our species met a premature death from the virus, less than half a century ago. This was a rupture in our human story at least as significant as the development of agriculture or the harnessing of fossil fuels, and just as unforeseen. Yet it is one which our species has yet to digest, owing to the chaos that ensued in its aftermath. Tonight, may we reconcile ourselves, one way or another, with our shared history, for if we cannot understand the past, we cannot understand the present.

Our purpose, then, our reason for coming together, is to share our insights and interpretations, our stories and our sadness, in the hope of moving into the future with a clearer understanding of the events which have shaped our collective situation. But, of course, this will not be an easy conversation, and I can already sense the tension and trepidation in the air.

Have you heard it too? The rainbow bee-eater sings of how, in the old cities of Empire, orchids now grow in the decomposing bodies of the dead. Can there be poetry after the Great Die-Off? Must there only be poetry after the Great Die-Off? What does it mean to be human in the wake of this colossal event? Some say we should be grateful for this dark tragedy; others condemn it as the most horrific stain on our collective story. These questions are not for me to answer and perhaps they have no answer. I pose them only to initiate our meditations, to stir the Great Spirit within, as we begin the formidable task of digesting our tragic history. Perhaps the truth of our condition lies not in providing answers to our questions but simply in the questioning itself. We may not find, but let us seek.

To what end, then, do we gather? The impulse is simple. We cannot fully understand an event or perspective until we have given it the opportunity to be discussed in the best and clearest light, just as we cannot be confident in what we believe until we have listened deeply to a range of counter-positions. Closing our minds to alternative modes of reasoning, knowing, or being, is evidence only of weakness and cowardice. We must move toward, not shy away from, that which unsettles us, for we are not weak, and we are not cowards.

That which unsettles make us stronger.

So this evening, as we welcome in the darkness, I call upon each of you to let down your guard and enter a place of open-minded vulnerability. For this discussion to take place we must look behind the blind fields in our vision, dissolve our prejudices and presuppositions, and be open to receiving and digesting uncomfortable truths. Let us seek not to confirm what we already believe but instead to refine our outlook; to muddle our way toward a deeper understanding of the issues under consideration; to follow the logic of sound reasoning wherever it may take us, however difficult or frightening the conclusions may be.

We could do no better than follow Socrates—after whom the Hemlock virus was named—and approach this discussion in a spirit where we would be pleased to be refuted and delivered from false consciousness. Accordingly, may we be enriched by whatever we hear this evening, whether the words are received in agreement or disagreement, and may we listen respectfully and with charity, trusting that we shall leave with sharper minds for having rubbed them against stones of various textures. On this journey, beneath this Red Magnetic Moon, may the Great Spirit give courage to us all.

In closing, let me make a brief comment on our ceremonial process. Tonight we will hear first from Immanuel Wright, who has agreed to sketch a rough, introductory picture of the Great Die-Off. We invite him as our inaugural speaker because he has spent recent years writing a *History of the Great Die-Off*, although this evening he tells me his address will not be a scholarly lecture but rather a personal account of the Great Die-Off, as he experienced it. Casting our minds back may be particularly valuable for our young, who did not live through those times. Immanuel will also be the first to speak on behalf of the victims and pass his own judgement on what took place.

After Immanuel has spoken, I will invite Durruk Senjen to speak. As you all know very well, this man is the last surviving member of the group who released Hemlock-42 into the world. It is critical that we hear his perspective, as this accords with the ancient principles of natural justice, which hold that individuals be given a fair hearing to defend or explain their actions.

In the spirit of critical inquiry, others will then be given the opportunity to assess the logic of any defence or prosecution that is offered, and tribal leaders have spent the day selecting a representative group of speakers, who may approach this task however they see fit. I only ask that speakers come to the centre where I stand, before this great fire, so that your voice can be heard by all. I know that many of us are ill practised at public discourse and that each of you deserves your day to be heard. I hope that there will be time for that, if not tonight, then in coming days. But for now, we need to begin the discussion and learn to listen to each other.

As seekers of wisdom and peace, I hope that we can hear from as many different people as possible tonight. If a speaker represents your perspective, please communicate your assent in a way that respects Dadirri. The task before us is immense. We need to ask whether the acts of Durruk Senjen and his conspirators were just or unjust. Should we pass judgement on and sentence them? Do we have the power or even the authority to do that? How should we digest our shared history? No doubt other questions will emerge from our difficult discussion in the hours, days, and weeks to come.

My friends, I have said all that is needed by way of grounding our ceremony. Thank you for your generous attention so far. Let me now call upon our first speaker, Immanuel Wright. By way of introduction he will provide more detail on the story of our sacred demise, and share, for our critical assessment, his opening judgement on those who released the virus. We ask our speakers to express themselves as simply as possible but with as much complexity as is necessary. Tonight, if the four winds be willing, let us communicate and think without filters.

Three times let us pray:

Blue Star, We are Thy Tears, The Guidance of Gaia, We Seek;
Great Spirit, the Fire in our Eyes, Before Thee, We Speak.

3. ECO-TERRORISM

Zola Eblo resumes her seat at the front of the assembled. Her final prayer hangs in the air as Immanuel Wright makes his way to the front of the fire. He has prepared for this moment for many weeks, almost fanatically, knowing his insides would continue burning until he had this opportunity to speak his mind and lay down his prosecution. In his imagination Immanuel is confident, articulate, and able to sway the crowd with his reasoned arguments. But when it comes time to speak, his voice catches.

Before him, in the shifting shadows of the crowd, he sees a mirage of his wife and child who were amongst the first victims of the virus. He remembers sweat, cold flannels, perplexed doctors and the moment when his daughter's hand went limp in his. More than anything he feels guilt. Guilt that he survived while so many perished. Guilt that he could not protect his family and that he has wasted the years since the Great Die-Off. What has he done since that time? Wallowed in self-pity. He had survived but he was a shadow of his former self. Often his guilt evolves into anger and bitterness, eating him up from the inside. But tonight, he is strangely numb, as if the intensity of the moment has led to a sensory overload and shutdown.

In the Before Time, Immanuel was a lawyer who modelled himself on the orator Cicero. Like his great predecessor, Immanuel learned his craft by the sea and was taught to bring his voice above the sound of crashing waves. He had screamed into those waves many times since. But as he stands in the silence his training comes back to him like muscle memory. Once again, he pushes down his grief and speaks.

People of the land, children of Gaia, my name is Immanuel Wright. Whether through lived experience or through story, we all know the circumstances that preceded the Great Die-Off. It sometimes felt that all we ever did was collect data on the environmental crisis. Of course, we have lost most of that science and analysis now, but we know the general predicament. Our civilisation had shot through all the ecological boundaries and squandered our inheritance of ancient sunlight. Inequalities in wealth distribution were perverse. We elected TV personalities to lead us and numbed ourselves with consumption and on-demand television. And still the material demands of our species continued to rise, even or especially amongst the richest sectors of global society.

But it was not all bad—people tend to forget that now. Progressive action was painfully slow, I admit, but a collective rumbling of resistance could be heard by the attentive listener. Sure, the naysayers complained that every small step forward was insignificant in the face of the many problems, but that missed the point. Ambition was to be ratcheted up over time; and let us not forget that social movements were mobilising and large sums of money—hundreds of billions of dollars—were shifting out of fossil fuels and into renewable energy... or energy as we call it now. We were making progress and things were beginning to change. But I guess it was easier to throw stones from the sideline than engage in the hard work of shifting industrial society onto a sustainable footing. History is made by people who try to achieve impossible things, just as history is lost by those who forego the struggle.

Those were dark days—but there were darker days to come. We all remember where we were when we heard that the mysterious Hemlock-42 had been released. I was driving my daughter to her basketball game when a song on the radio—'Amused to Death' by Roger Waters—was interrupted with a breaking news bulletin. I can still hear the lady's voice as she reported that 542 people had been found dead on the east coast of the United States. Many more deaths followed and it was clear that health authorities were in a panic and were desperately trying to contain the outbreak. We know now that their efforts were in vain; they did not stand a chance.

The virus spread like a lightning plague and it was not hard for preachers around the world to convince masses of terrified people that the end times had come—didn't God promise not a flood, but a fire next time? But this was no act of God. Human beings did this. And they even gave it a clever name, 'Hemlock-42'.

I laughed bitterly at this reference to the poison given to the greatest of Western philosophers. Didn't they know that Socrates died needlessly, as a result of false accusations? He was given a choice—death or go into exile. And *he chose* to die. He was an old man, as far as we know. No doubt he hoped that his act would be romanticised by his infatuated pupil, Plato. Whatever the case, the point is Socrates made that choice for himself, not for other people. Did those murderers in the faction of the Association of Concerned Earth Scientists really think it appropriate to name their virus after a man who said that we have 'only one thing to consider in performing any action: whether we are acting justly or unjustly, like a good person or a bad one'? Will those who defend the murder of innocent people stand before us today and declare themselves good people? I don't think so. They wouldn't dare. A defence of genocide for reason X only sets a precedent for some other group of vigilantes to justify genocide for reason Y. We may be fallen creatures but let us not fall to those depths.

But what does any of that matter now? We don't have the luxury of philosophy today. The only mercy was that Hemlock-42 took the young and old quickly. Every single one of the innocent fallen deserve to have their story told and to sit in judgement of those responsible. Today we only refer to them as a number—an estimated 7.8 billion lost; 7.8 billion murdered. It sounds so abstract, doesn't it? But they each had names, lives, families, worries, and hopes for the future. Think especially of the children whose innocent lives were so callously taken from them. We can't hear from them all but, if you will indulge me, I want to tell you something about my daughter,

Fin. Her memory is all I have left and there are parts of her character and nature I will keep to myself. The murderers don't deserve to know her.

My wife and I never wanted to have children. The future felt so uncertain and we would stay up late into the night debating whether it was cruel to bring another person into the world. Most of our friends did not have children and the birth rate was falling in most countries worldwide. But then she came. She was unplanned but not unloved. Our moralising gave way to the necessity of caring for this utterly dependent being that had interrupted our lives.

Most parents are proud of their children and I am no exception. Fin grew into a strong and resilient girl. She learned the names of all the flowers and trees in our area. She tended a vegetable patch and swapped food with our neighbours. Her laugh was music. I spoke with her about climate change but only in generalities. Back then those with privilege could hide the worst things from their kids. They could keep them 'innocent'. But that is also something we can't do anymore. Fin joined marches and demonstrations with hundreds of other children. We painted banners together and I can remember her leaning over our table, her tongue poking out of the corner of her mouth as she concentrated on lettering: 'The Oceans Are Rising and So Are We!'

When we heard the virus had reached our country, we packed our bags and headed to our holiday house near the beach. We did not have time to plan but we thought we could stay there and wait it out; wait for the virus to pass over us. When she got a fever, we hoped it was just a cold. Kids get sick all the time. After a few days I thought she was starting to get better. She crawled out of bed one evening and sat in my arms and we talked for hours—just like old times. Maybe I should have sent her back to bed. But I thought the fever had lifted and I missed her laugh. The next morning her virus was back with a vengeance. Nothing we tried worked and she could not keep any liquids down. Fin was already slight but each day she lost weight and conditioning. Her eyes were shockingly bloodshot; I swear her skin was turning grey and her voice grew weaker... until one day she slipped away. We buried her six feet deep. A foot for every year of her beautiful life. My sweet daughter; my only child. Gone forever.

Death was all around us at that time. The world was in chaos; the markets were crashing. There was no time for grief and, besides, who could listen to our pain? Show me a person who was not also in anguish. So, we pushed it down and got on with the business of surviving, despite everything.

I tell you this not so that you will feel sorry for me. I don't want your pity. This is our lives now and it is long overdue for us to sit in judgement of the murderers and terrorists, one of whom sits amongst us today. I tell you this story because the experience of loss crystallised something in my mind. It provided a foundation upon which I can say that the killing of even one innocent person is a moral wrong. It is never ok to take human life or to use a human being as a means to an end. Old philosophers would have called it radical evil. All peoples and all cultures have understood this. It is the one moral truth that people have always agreed on. Even Adolf Hitler tried to justify his slaughter of the Jews through propaganda and crude speeches. But who is Hitler next to people like Durruk Senjen, the prime orchestrator of the Great Die-Off? Hitler's gas installations look like simple toys next to what he and his collaborators did. A terrorist is no less a terrorist just because he or she is motivated by ecological salvation.

I know what Senjen will say in response: that they acted for some abstract notion of 'justice' or the 'greater good'; that we are lucky to be alive on this flourishing Earth. Maybe. But after all that has happened, most days I wish I were dead. And it did not feel lucky when I was lowering first, my daughter, and then my wife, into the ground—lowering them into makeshift graves that I dug with my own sweat and tears. And it is precisely that image that I want you to hold in your mind. I want you to think about someone you lost during the Great Die-Off. Hold them in your mind, in their beautiful uniqueness. Remember their smile and their laughter. Because the only question before us today is this: *are you in favour of bringing the murderers to justice or are you against it?* I for one cannot abide the thought of these people roaming free in our community.

That it was unjust to murder billions of innocents needs no further proof. To argue the case further would impart upon the terrorists a dignity they do not deserve. Let us just acknowledge what is perfectly obvious: the release of Hemlock-42 was the vilest act in the history of our species. It was a harrowing violation of human rights—and that murderer, Durruk Senjen, should pay for his horrendous sins with his life. And I hope his collaborators are burning in the depths of hell.

With that Immanuel Wright storms away from the fire pit and resumes his seat. There is a quiet murmur amongst those gathered as people share immediate reactions with their neighbours. Zola Eblo is seen gathering twigs and branches from around the fire pit into a pile, before raising her hand for silence and inviting the next speaker to address the assembly.

4. Delusions of Non-Violence

There is palpable tension in the air as Professor Durruk Senjen—former chair of the Association of Concerned Earth Scientists—is called to address the crowd. People cast their eyes around trying to see the new speaker approach but for a long time he does not appear. The crowd begins to get restless, wondering whether he will show up at all, but soon people fall quiet and a division in the crowd opens up as an old man walks silently toward the centre of the amphitheatre.

With shadows dancing around him, Professor Senjen looks people in the eye as he moves, not showing any signs of shame or intimidation. There are occasional outbursts from the crowd of 'murderer' or 'evil beast', and someone throws an object which strikes the side of Senjen's face, although the old man does not flinch as he wipes away the blood from his cheek. But generally people are peaceful and reserved, somewhat stunned at being in the presence of this individual who had achieved a certain mythical notoriety through the stories that had been told over the decades. For the first time they realise that he is not a myth but a man—now an old man—who looked like any other, of flesh and blood.

As he reaches the fire, he pauses, turns to the crowd, lifts his eyes and hands to the sky and screams an almighty scream, barely human in tone, which echoes around the stadium. The scream unleashed is an alchemy of dark emotions—grief, pain, anger, and unspeakable sorrow. It startles the crowd and yet everyone remains quiet, apprehensively waiting for what would come next. Senjen's eyes fall to the people before him, he breathes deeply, and begins to speak slowly and deliberately.

Beneath these stars, I see you; before this fire, I feel you. My name is Durruk Senjen. Although you owe me nothing, tonight I ask for your openness, for I cannot be understood if I do not have your openness. I thank Zola for her graceful welcome, and I thank Immanuel, our first speaker, for the frankness of his speech, condemning though it was.

You will discover soon enough that, although I stand before you a frail old man, I am a creature of passion and conviction and, old though I am, my mind is as sharp as it has ever been. My ears hear all too well. Yes, I collaborated on the development of Hemlock-42, and I participated with others in its intentional release. For decades I have felt the exile and the burden. This evening I have heard the whispers and the taunts. Even now I can see the hatred in the eyes of some of you, as you cast your shallow and venomous judgements. We have just heard from Immanuel Wright, so confident in his conviction of my actions—and who could not empathise with his painful account of loss? My eyes are still wet.

At the same time, I found his prosecution to be a gross simplification and distortion of the bigger picture; so narrow in its line of sight and so limited in its understanding of context. It was merely an emotional outpouring—quite understandably so, and I sincerely hope he found it therapeutic. But if we are to understand our history, we need analysis. Tonight, I have been given the opportunity to respond to my detractors and, for that, I am indebted to you all.

Without intending any disrespect, it does not appear to me that Immanuel was competent to undertake the task he set himself. On the face of things his conviction may appear convincing to the uncritical thinker—no doubt many here sympathised with his heartfelt prosecution. But this evening it will become clear that his take on things is erroneous in many questions of fact, and unhinged and misguided in so many questions of evaluation. Sometimes a partial view of things can distort the entire picture, evoking a mirage of truth or clarity when really there are only falsities and confusions.

So I say to you all: be wary of those, like Immanuel, who are quick to simplify what is complex or who use pithy statements of 'truth' rather than rational arguments. For when complex things seem simple, it may be that it is ye who is simple. Tonight, we must be prepared to look beneath the surface of things and not follow the herd of unthinking critics to commonsensical but mistaken conclusions about our history. The issues under consideration are too important for knee-jerk responses. But be warned, you must be prepared to hear things you may not want to hear, for that is what lies ahead, I am sure.

Before I respond to the substance of Immanuel's critique and expose the elementary but critical errors in his reasoning and assessment, indulge me for a moment, if you will, as I tell you a story from my boyhood. The night is young and we have time. Besides, the relevance will become clear soon enough.

I grew up in a small town—less than 60 kilometres north of this derelict city in which we find ourselves tonight—whose main industry was textile production. It was a precarious industry, the last in my locality which had not been outsourced to Asia to exploit the cheapness of the labour and weakness of environmental regulations. There was always the threat of our factories closing, too, which would have reduced our humble settlement to an economic dead-spot like so many rural towns had become, as industries moved overseas in pursuit of greater profits. Naturally we felt grateful for our industry, mundane though it was, for it was our community's primary livelihood.

Both my parents worked in the largest factory in the town, my father rising to the position of shift manager. We had a relatively comfortable though somewhat insecure existence, and although my parents found little sense of satisfaction in their working lives, and their working hours were extremely demanding, we were happy enough in our family life. For the most part I can say I enjoyed a happy childhood. My friends and I spent most of the afternoons after school and weekends down by the local waterhole, within walking distance from my home. This was a wondrous though humble natural treasure, and a source of sensuous relief for us all, especially as we found the summers getting longer and more intense. My friendship group grew up together down at the waterhole, swimming through childhood and becoming young adults under the gentle guidance of the river's flow.

At some point, however, the state of things at our sanctuary began to change. At first it was the water developing a new, distinct smell of chemicals, and occasionally it would appear tainted with colour— reds, blues, and greens, depending on the day. The changes were so gradual or sporadic, however, that they almost escaped notice, such that there came a time when we could barely remember the crystal clarity of earlier times. Had the water ever been clean and clear? We used to squeal with a mixture of shock and delight as we felt an eel or fish brush past our submerged bodies, but over time this happened less and less, until one day we realised that it never happened anymore. Had it ever happened? Didn't we once see and hear birds? Not anymore. Even our dogs would no longer dive ecstatically into the waterhole as they used to, and they would never drink from it, as if they knew something we didn't. Then again, perhaps we knew very well that our waterhole was dying, and we just didn't have the courage to admit it, plain though it was to see.

It wasn't until we started getting sick that any of us mentioned this to our parents. I remember missing weeks of school when I was 14 or 15, recovering only to fall sick again, a phenomenon that I shared with many of my friends. One summer evening I mentioned to my father that I wondered whether the sickness was due to the water we were swimming in, which seemed to spark something in his mind, or lift it from his subconscious. The next Sunday afternoon, after his shift at work, he accompanied me down to the waterhole and for the first time in years he saw the state of the water we had been swimming in. I recall watching his face as he assessed the situation—it was as if he were repressing a scream, and I noticed his eyes become glassy and threaten to release a tear. His face braced stoically and he called on me to return home with him. No words were spoken.

Later I learned that my father confronted senior management about this, knowing his factory was responsible for this ruin of the waterhole, but his voice was silenced with the threat of losing his job if he 'rocked the boat'. It turns out that to save costs the chemical by-product of the industry was being released into the river upstream, which had led to the toxic smell and unusual colour of the water. The local council turned a blind eye to this violation of regulations for fear of undermining the economic heart of the town. Likewise, my father, needing to maintain an income to pay the mortgage and put food on the table, felt obliged to keep overseeing the workers who were responsible for the chemical discharge, although plainly this work was tearing him up inside. My mother, unable to show my father's restraint, ended up being 'let go' for objecting to the industrial waste practices, placing my family in a precarious financial position.

My group of friends were banned from swimming in the waterhole, and over the years my occasional visits to the area would only expose an ever more upsetting image of a toxic pond, with slime and oils on the surface and the water increasingly littered with plastic bottles and aluminium cans. The whole area began to smell so pungent it was barely tolerable. The waterhole, which had been a quiet source of spiritual nourishment to me and my friends, had become a lifeless wasteland, but this death was not merely external. I no longer felt quite at home in the world. Something inside me had died.

One consequence was that as my teenage years ticked over I spent less and less time outdoors or with friends, disconnected both from nature and my community of peers. When my closest friend, Henry, died of cancer at 17, I dealt with this by drinking more than I should have, as if I were searching for something irreplaceable that had been lost. If I am honest, I was trying to distract myself from thoughts of suicide. A stronger character might have reacted differently, but I made my decisions and must live with them. I was adrift in the cosmos without meaning or direction. My soul was empty and alone. On the flip side, my father received a promotion and a raise, as faster fashion cycles had led to increased profits for the factory.

I tell you this story to provide a specific and tangible example of a general tendency in what was called industrial civilisation. I suspect most of you have your own such story to tell, personal tales of ecological loss and grief, of shattered communities, forgotten dreams, and the lost sense of wonder. Perhaps the older amongst you still remember the strange ache of alienated life in the midst of industrial society. I am confident in this suspicion because I have come to understand the inner logic of industrial civilisation, a cold and uncompromising logic that ruthlessly sought profit maximisation at the expense of people and planet. Be perfectly clear, the industrial form of life was not able to respect its ecological foundations. It was destructive of nature, by nature. And this was also reflected in the tragic inner dimension of human life. Too often the lack of meaning and purpose in life produced social neuroses that manifested in violence, greed, narcissism, consumerism, and an ever-present sense of latent anguish.

The details of my story are unique but by the turn of the 21st century the basic story of natural degradation and social alienation was well-nigh universal. Even those few individuals who were supposedly 'winning' the rat race carried faces twisted with despair and quiet desperation, to say nothing of the great multitudes in debilitating poverty whose interests had been cast aside and ignored to serve market demands of the rich. I remember when I was in my late twenties, just as I was coming out of a depressive episode and discovering a love of biochemistry as a PhD candidate, I learnt that six men owned more wealth than the poorest half of humanity. How does one digest such a statistic? Why did we not explode with rage and indignation?

As it happened, we humans were all so numb or distracted or consumed by a sense of powerlessness that no one revolted and few resisted. Instead, our species seemed to have resigned itself to a tragic fate, a fate a novelist once described as 'a boot stamping on a human face—forever'. The lucky ones merely amused themselves to death. I found amusement—or rather neurotic distraction—in the study of viruses, and by accident of history I found myself one day, rather early in my academic career, on the board of the Association of Concerned Earth Scientists, about which, of course, I shall have more to say shortly.

Global capitalism had become the dominant form of social organisation and it was brutal in its methods for self-preservation and expansion, not a tool serving human interests but a force of its own requiring both the servitude of growing portions of humanity and an ever-increasing demand of natural resources to be thrown into the furnace of growth. It is wrong even to characterise this system 'anthropocentric', since that would imply it merely privileging human interests over ecological ones. No, this system was 'capitalocentric', for it cared as little for human wellbeing as it did for environmental wellbeing. Both were mere resources for profit-maximisation, and both were expendable. Sure, spectacular technologies were developing and more people were leaving their peasant life for a 'progressive' urban existence, but as one early critic wrote, we did not ride upon the railroad, it rode upon us.

And so, to begin my formal response, the first of Immanuel's errors can now be addressed more directly. He spoke with apparent sincerity of environmental harm and made passing acknowledgements to his concerns about social injustice. A good start, so far as it went. But his brief and superficial rendering of these problems served only to disguise or perhaps deliberately hide the nature and extent of the true contradictions facing humanity in the Age of Empire. We were pursuing infinite growth on a finite planet, a recipe for disaster that a four-year-old could discern. But our economists defended this as the only model of progress, and our politicians hired them to design our economies. Apparently, there was no alternative.

Earth had come to resemble a giant petri dish, in which the dominant colony of human bacteria was in the process of consuming all available resources and poisoning itself from its own wastes. You may find this analogy polemical and over-stated, but I am not in the business of hyperbole; I seek and demand accuracy and honesty. Humanity had become a plague. Do not forget that when Hemlock-42 was released on that fateful day, in December 2027, the human population had risen to 8.4 billion—growing at 200,000 people *every day*. Nearly every one of those individuals was living within globalised systems of production and cultures of consumption that celebrated material affluence as the path to happiness and contentment in life. It was the measure of societal progress and personal success. But the material and energetic demands we were making on planetary ecosystems were brutal and ultimately unbearable. Is it any wonder that scientists back then warned of the vanishing face of Gaia?

For many people the personal experience of this unfolding ecological apocalypse was hidden from sight by virtue of their artificial and insulated urban existence. Granted, the cities of industrial civilisation were always tending toward destruction and pollution, but early on people had become habituated to their urban wastelands. When one grows up in a concrete jungle devoid of life one is rarely able to appreciate what has been lost; and one cannot love what one does not know. Although people watched the corporate news and followed social media, which occasionally reported of environmental disturbances, the real devastation was hidden by the fact that most of the damage was occurring out of the cities, in order to import materials to the belching and consumptive urban environments.

Globally, our great forests were being destroyed; our rivers and oceans were being polluted with plastics and chemicals; great vessels were casually trawling the ocean floor with devastating results; our soils—the foundation of any civilisation—were being mined to dust and poisoned through practices of industrial agriculture and left to blow away in the wind as the next frontier was sought. Our extravagant squandering of fossil fuels was upsetting the climatic balance, leading to harsher climates and more extreme weather events—floods, cyclones, droughts—impacting the poorest regions first and hardest while the rich sat comfortably inside with the air conditioning on. That said, ultimately ecosystemic instability was pretty democratic in its impact, brutalising nations rich and poor without caring much for national income. As a tragic aside, all of this was leading to a holocaust of biodiversity of unbearable severity, leading some to declare we were living through the Sixth Great Extinction. Indeed, we were.

And so, to bring my first point home, Immanuel's framing of the ecological predicament was fundamentally misconceived by being grossly understated, and, with respect, he did a disservice to our ceremony this evening to mislead you all as he did. When one's house is ablaze, we must not speak of candles! We must panic and act! The violence done to Gaia in the name of economic progress was not an unfortunate mistake that could be remedied through reform, but an inescapable feature of a system compelled to grow for the sake of growth, like a cancer cell. And like a cancer cell, Empire was killing its host, Earth; just as a parasite feeds off its own life-support system; just like the snake that eats its own tail to nourish itself as it kills itself. Gaia was dying, or rather, being killed. Let that be perfectly clear.

Do not forget that all this was happening despite the voices of reason emerging from the environmental movement, of which I became a part through my role with the Association of Concerned Earth Scientists. For all intents and purposes the environmental movement was a despairing failure, but not through lack of good intentions. Decades of green censure and calls for 'sustainable consumption' had not stemmed the tide of overconsumption, at most they had mitigated middleclass guilt. The deeper systemic problem was that industrial civilisation was extractivist by nature. It did not know how to stop producing more and more, let alone contract or 'degrow' toward sufficiency, and in fact growth was considered the solution to the crises growth was causing.

Small environmental wins were gratefully embraced—temporarily protecting a forest here; a wetland there—but only the wilfully blind missed the fact that for every win there were a thousand losses. Empire marched on despite every protest and despite every attempt at resistance, and soon enough the apocalypse had been normalised.

Crisis was no longer something to avoid in the future but something we were living through. Yet, like fish that did not know they were in water, most people could not see it, since it had become the fabric of existence. Life went on and politicians began to learn the art of paying lip service to environmental issues—and all the while the carrying capacity of the planet continued its steep and inexorable decline.

Nevertheless, for one to frame Empire primarily as an ecological catastrophe is to miss the broader nature of this mode of industrial existence. In order to provide affluent living standards for a minority of the global population, the rich nations needed to invest significant portions of their wealth in militarisation. Indigenous communities do not voluntarily give up their forests and lands and resources for exportation or occupation, so violence, or the threat of violence, was needed to secure the necessary flow of resources. Through colonialisation the rich nations took what they needed, first through military force and slavery, then through economic coercion and duress, as market power came to reduce (without eliminating) the need for cruder forms of violence, theft, and oppression. The colonists considered this a process of 'civilising' primitive cultures, for the good of the primitives, of course—an ideological pill which I am sure no one was sincerely able to swallow. It was theft backed by violence, plain and simple. When indigenous peoples fought back—indeed, when anyone fought back—they were killed or put in jail for violating the new laws of the land. People and nations fell in line or were eliminated.

This brings me now to the heart of my response to the first prosecutor, who spoke with such conviction about how my actions, and the actions of my collaborators, were a violation of human rights. Perhaps they were a violation. Please be sure I am not here to disguise or downplay the horror of the Great Die-Off. Nor am I going to deny in any way my role in instigating it. And while I am also not here to apologise for my actions you must accept that I am haunted and tormented everyday by the unfathomable pain and suffering I caused to so many through my deliberate actions. Do not for a moment deny me that horror and grief—I know that I took your wife and child from you, Mr Wright. I know they suffered, and I know you suffered and still suffer because they suffered. I screamed for them and I screamed for you. I scream for all of you. And I scream for myself.

But if we are to speak of rights, we must also ask difficult questions about whose rights we are referring to and what happens when rights conflict. Do only the rights of humans count, as Immanuel Wright implies? Is Earth merely a resource for our single species to do with what we wish, the broader community of life be damned? What about the rights of the laughing owl and the leatherback turtle that co-exist on this beautiful planet? And what of the generations to come, human or otherwise, who would wish to be born into environmental conditions that are conducive to flourishing? At the very least, I ask you to reject the naïve clarity of our first speaker and recognise that these are complex issues in a fraught and ambiguous moral terrain.

I could pose the issue another way: If you are polluting a river, would it be a violation of your rights if someone intervened to protect the health of the waterways and the fish that inhabit them? In my view, use of force, if necessary, would be justifiable to protect the rights of nature from your violence; and to protect the rights of future human generations to enjoy that river, unpolluted. The river and the fish cannot fight back, nor can generations yet unborn. It follows that others must step up as guardians—not out of choice but out of duty—to protect the rights of the weak against the interests of the powerful. This is the central implication of a moral order in which rights are recognised and respected. Nobody in good conscience can claim a right that involves undermining natural systems needed for the entire community of life.

I ask you to consider, then, if you have the mental courage, that my actions were intended not to violate rights but to protect them—not only human rights, now and of the future, but the rights of our sentient brothers and sisters of the animal kingdom, and even the rights of rivers to flow cleanly and forests to grow and provide homes to the millions of other species we share this sublime planet with, now and in the future. As we all know, scientists offered a humble 'warning to humanity' in 1992, warning that our species was on a collision course with the natural world. Yet nothing changed and indeed the path of destruction only intensified. A second warning was offered in 2017 and again, things only got worse. A third warning was offered in 2027, and yet again desperate calls for change were accompanied by spineless inaction. Empire would not lie down like a lamb at the polite request of left-leaning environmental scientists. It knew only how to devour anything that stood in its way.

So, should we have waited for more evidence? Should we have released a fourth and fifth warning, saying the same thing with even more compelling evidence? Should we have called on more people to recycle, take shorter showers, and lobby their politicians to invest more in conservation programmes and renewable energy? It is my view that, from a rational-scientific perspective, we had more than enough evidence in the 1970s to see that the path of industrialisation was chronically unsustainable and in need of fundamental transformation; and since the 1970s, if not much earlier, we had well-meaning environmentalists campaigning for 'green living', 'green growth', and 'green policy', all with negligible influence. The machine did not and could not relent. Thus, by the early decades of the 21st century the evidential case for ecological collapse was terrifyingly compelling. Earth was under assault. What would another scientific report or warning do? Earth and its creatures were being murdered, day by day, and everybody knew it. Surely no civilisation had as much evidence of their impending collapse as we did.

At what point, then, was one entitled to say that the threshold had been passed; that the attempts to slow the beast down were not working and would not work? At what point was a person entitled to try to bring the beast down rather than watch it destroy everything he loved? If you disagree with the line my collaborators and I drew in the sand, fine, but at least state your threshold! When 90% of the tropical rainforests had been cut down? 95%? Name your threshold! Too many people, even the most passionate and compassionate environmentalists, just sat by thinking the same old strategies would eventually win out, but while they wallowed in such naïve hope the Western black rhino went extinct—forever—as did an estimated 200 other species, *every day*.

My collaborators and I came to realise that the machine of industrial civilisation was unreformable and that all attempts to solve environmental problems through lifestyle change, political campaigning, and technological innovation were destined for failure. We did not want to involve ourselves in activities that felt good, seemed sensible, or merely mitigated our guilt. We could not stomach writing another report detailing the catastrophes unfolding only to have it ignored. We wanted to *achieve our goals* of creating ecological balance on Earth. That is what drove us to be scientists in the first place—our love of nature. That meant we had to meditate more deeply on the question of strategy, to adjust our strategies depending on what might actually work, and we were brave enough to follow the logic of our reasoning through to the most disturbing of conclusions. Timider souls would no doubt have turned away and returned to their gardens to pass their time fiddling while Gaia burned. But we looked truth in the eye without flinching and never turned away. History will be on our side.

In short, there was only one way to restore ecological balance on Earth. Industrial civilisation had to be destroyed and the human population needed to be radically downscaled. On that premise, the only remaining question was how to achieve this as quickly as possible. I initiated discussions with others on the board of ACES who I believed were sympathetic to this line of reasoning and together we developed Hemlock-42 to execute our plans. With the death of billions of people, now the Earth and her creatures regenerate before our eyes. The great forests are returning; the rivers and soils are healing; the air hasn't been this fresh for many hundreds of years; and best of all, Earth is again teeming with life as the Great Rewilding gets underway. It is beautiful, sublime. I am glad to the point of tears. And even if your conscious minds cannot yet accept it, deep down you know that Earth is grateful for my radical and desperate intervention; and deep down you know that, because of my actions, our species now has a chance to thrive into the deep future in balance and harmony. My colleagues and I carried the cross for the sins of our species and now we all have a chance at a second life.

Many of you, I know very well, reproach us as murderers and villains. But consider, if you have the courage, that we *acted out of love*. If you cannot understand that, you cannot understand much that I have to say. We destroyed in order to conserve—not because we despised humankind but because we love nature, upon which we all depend. So next time you delight in the song of the rainbow bee-eater or drink from a clean river, you are welcome to share your gratitude. But please spare me your simple condemnations.

In closing, I make no apologies and seek no forgiveness for my actions, horrid though they were. Like Socrates, I will accept any sentence you lay down, but I will not accept any baseless verdict of guilt. Indeed, to correct Immanuel Wright's misinterpretation, we referenced the poison of Hemlock when naming our virus knowing that we would be unjustly condemned for our noble actions. So be sure, I have looked into my dark soul and made peace, knowing that if I had my time again, I would not change my path. Who amongst you was ever prepared to gaze into the mirror of your own existence and look yourself squarely in the eye? I am accused of unspeakable violence, but your self-image of non-violence is nothing but a pathetic delusion. Every day the lives of the 'ordinary consumer' contributed to ecological annihilation and every day such consumers refused to plumb the depths of their subconscious to see this. My violence was explicit and calculated. Theirs was insidious and causal—and infinitely more dangerous for being so.

Why, then, am I on trial this evening, rather than those who did nothing to stop the onslaught? I put it to you all that this entire ceremony needs to be deconstructed, for doing *nothing* was criminal;

doing *nothing* was a violation of rights! If anything, I should be the judge—the judge-penitent—if only because I saw our collective guilt so plainly and had the guts to act in reconciliation. Thus I call on you, passive bystanders—no, you passive assassins—to defend the charge of aiding and abetting ecocide! I know my judgement of you in advance. I condemn you. I condemn you!

For a moment there is silence, but soon the crowd erupts loudly in response, although the balance of support is entirely unclear. The cacophony of spirited discussion is maintained for several minutes before slowly fading as Durruk Senjen returns to the shadows from where he came. Distracted by her own troubled thoughts, Zola neglects her role as facilitator for a time, staring at the ground before her. Eventually the next speaker takes the initiative and moves to stand before the assembly, without Zola's formal invitation.

5. Resistance and Democracy

Mohandria Bentharma is an elder now—she is known to most people simply as Aunty—but prior to the Great Die-Off she was a youthful and energetic social justice activist, working on the nexus of climate change and health. As the climate warmed it became clear that the operating space of vector-borne diseases (especially malaria) was expanding, putting vast new populations at risk of infection. What provoked Mohandria into activism was the knowledge that so many of the deaths from such diseases could be prevented with devices as simple and cheap as the mosquito net. And yet, disturbingly, the provision of mosquito nets seemed to be an unaffordable expense in a world that had other priorities.

Overflowing with empathy for the suffering poor, Mohandria could not sit by as thousands upon millions of people died every year, mostly children, for want of a $1 mosquito net. Consequently, as a nineteen-year-old university student she founded a grassroots movement which pressured governments and philanthropists around the world to invest in the free provision of mosquito nets to populations at risk of malaria and similar diseases. The methods of this movement included practices of non-violent civil disobedience, most famously when almost two thousand activists occupied and ultimately shut down the World Economic Forum at Davos in 2022. Due to police brutality, media attention turned the event into an embarrassment for the world leaders, who had little option but to act decisively in the face of public backlash. A global fund of $5 billion dollars was established from a mixture of public and private donations, and within two years free mosquito nets were available to anyone who needed them. It was estimated that almost one million lives were saved every year.

Of course, the work of social activism is never done. Mohandria continued to work passionately in various social and environmental domains, and by the time of the Great Die-Off she had achieved celebrity status globally as an inspired and inspiring change-maker. She has been invited to speak tonight on account of her lifelong dedication to advancing social justice through spirited activism.

This evening she moves slowly toward where she is to address the crowd. She is assisted by a walking stick, but something about her disposition makes it clear that there is still a fire burning in her eyes. She clears her throat and begins to speak, with a youthful vibrancy that defies her age.

Warm greetings, my brothers and sisters, on this cold and fateful night. My name is Mohandria Bentharma. I am humbled by this opportunity to address you all this evening. May the love of the Great Spirit be with you all.

Whether I can make a valuable contribution to this discussion remains to be seen, but I am inspired by the commitment to discourse and open debate that underpins our gathering this evening, for there is no other way for us to understand our moment in history. *Who* are we? *Where* are we? And what might we yet *become*? These are, of course, perennial human questions, but they lie at the foundation of our difficult inquiries tonight and how we answer them will define who we are. We are justified, therefore, in being intimidated and daunted by this ceremony, for nothing less than the collective soul of our species is at stake.

We have just heard the impassioned speech of Professor Senjen, who not only absolves himself and his colleagues of any guilt but concludes with accusations of the rest of us. His self-righteousness was abrasive and hard to swallow, but he did raise various points that ought to be given closer attention, and for that provocation let us offer him our thanks. After all, we are here to challenge each other. We may never arrive at the final and complete truth, but I assure you we can do better than the rhetorical offerings of Professor Senjen.

To be fair, one owes a certain respect to the raw emotion driving this man, for it seems he has genuinely convinced himself of the propriety of his own murderous acts, by dressing up his adolescent rage in the language of science and strategy. But any student of psychoanalysis can see that he represents a classic case of the Oedipal complex. As a child, Senjen was justifiably distraught when his father's actions destroyed his beloved swimming hole—his safe space—inducing feelings of fatherly hate and resentment, which he repressed, while his mother fought for its protection, inducing deeper feelings of love toward her. But as he left childhood and became a man this hate-love relationship merely took civilisational form, whereby Father Civilisation had to be killed in order to love Mother Earth. The Freudian insight that childhood experiences shape the adult finds no more compelling example. In a rather bitter twist of fate, however, one should note that Hemlock-42 took his mother's life while sparing his father's, no doubt casting more fuel into the furnace of his unbalanced psychology, which was on display this evening.

Indeed, you will have noticed that Professor Senjen's crude reasoning embodied a rather unsophisticated logic: *He hated what humans were doing; therefore, destroy humans.* Is there not something grossly ironic and contradictory here? The perpetrators so deeply resented the violence of humanity and so their response was to commit the most violent act in history! Sadly, I am reminded of the alcoholic who began drinking in the morning to ease the pain of his hangover. If, as the professor implied, there is a violence inherent to human nature, then he has merely taken that violent nature to its logical extreme, even as he conceives of himself as a hero and saviour, driven at the conscious level by feelings of love.

A hero—not at all. We never asked for him to save us through violence. He and his collaborators represent the most egregious form of the very arrogance and violence to which they claim to object. And the professor had the gall to call on us to look in the mirror! If he had truly looked in the mirror, he would have seen a confused and lost man who was no doubt genuinely grieving for the demise of nature and her species, but who was unable to channel that understandable grief into any positive intervention. Instead, his conservative life as an academic scientist repressed his rage and frustration such that it produced a neurosis of psychopathic dimensions. People did not pay sufficient attention to his manifesto, so he engaged in mass murder, as if there were no alternative strategies available. A less able scientist might have merely thrown a chemical bomb into a crowded room, but unfortunately the impressive ability of this ambitious but unstable biochemist led to the Great Die-Off. All the worse for humanity.

Are we to assume that the 42 in Hemlock-42 refers to the 'meaning of life' as stated in that old science fiction novel? I forget the name. What a tragic shame it is that this misguided scientist could only find meaning in his life through enacting violence. One is reminded of the football hooligans in the Before Time who would fight rival fans—only they were infinitely less ambitious. It was a world where human beings—especially young men, I am afraid—too often felt the need to brawl, beat women, go to war, or, in Senjen's case, commit mass murder, to find purpose and place in the world. If any of you think those are paths to prosperity, you have not yet thought hard enough. Hemlock-42 was nothing but a failure of imagination. Could he not rather have disengaged with the culture he despised and redirected his life energy to creating an alternative world that transcended rather than destroyed the existing order? At the very least, this prefigurative strategy could have bought that troubled civilisation in the Before Time a little more time to develop ethically and spiritually.

As some of you will know, I spent the best part of my adult life, prior to the Great Die-Off, as an activist seeking to protect vulnerable humans from easily preventable diseases. I never lived the life of a saint, believe me, but I did what I could, within my humble means. My activism was motivated by something deep in my moral constitution that told me it was wrong for so many human beings to suffer and have their lives cut short so unnecessarily, especially at a time when human wealth was so vast. In a rich world, the universal provision of food and water, of basic safety equipment, of medical care, would have been a minor inconvenience and their provision would have avoided great human suffering. One has a moral duty to act in such situations. And the richer the world got, the more unforgivable was the persistence of poverty.

You will understand, then, why I find it not just crude but offensive to be condemned by Professor Senjen. I spent my life fighting for progressive change, not without some success—fighting to help millions of vulnerable people avoid disease—only for this man to assume the authority to kill billions of human beings by deliberately exposing them to a fatal virus. If I were not so deeply trained in the Buddhist practices of mindfulness, I am sure, as I heard him speak tonight, that I would have mustered the energy and strength, despite my old age, to throw him in the fire without hesitation or remorse. But of course, that would be to reduce myself to his methods—methods steeped in violence which I unconditionally reject.

My emotions are unsettled, so let me pause for a moment. I must not allow my time here to degenerate into the shabby polemics of Professor Senjen. Having vented some of my anger and grief let me recompose myself and begin a more systematic and orderly critique of his so-called defence.

Let us begin by acknowledging the obvious: the actions of Senjen and his collaborators were elitist in the extreme. A small handful of scientists—justly concerned about the degradation of global ecosystems and the decline of species—took it into their hands, without public discussion, to release a virus that decimated the human population, including billions of innocent children. So wise and insightful was this group that they felt confident they knew what was best for our species and the planet we inhabit. So enlightened were they that they could see into the future and know what it held, despite the infinite variables that made such projections impossibly complex. And so self-aggrandising were they that they felt comfortable murdering billions but devised a virus that, in Senjen's case at least, spared himself. It was all obscene.

Of the seven perpetrators, only one—Dr Sophia McCabe—had the decency to kill herself the evening the virus was released, despite having a genetic immunity to Hemlock-42. It was an insufficient act of redemption but at least it was something. Five others of Senjen's team died from the virus itself, not having a genetic immunity. On the other hand, Senjen has tonight talked of the courage he needed to release the virus, but was silent about his own cowardice in choosing a fate for others that he would not accept for himself. After all, he knew in advance that he had a genetic immunity to the virus, and no doubt this knowledge shaped his actions.

Never could it be right for so few to assume the authority to assassinate the 'herd' of ordinary people to achieve some uncertain ecological salvation. This alone is enough to condemn Senjen and his disciples. Their guilt, I would have thought, was self-evident. Even those who sympathise with the noble goal of ecological restoration should be appalled by the elitist methods they chose to achieve their goals. What if those methods were used to pursue a goal you did not agree with? The gross and inexcusable procedural injustice renders the substantive goal beside the point.

This leads me to a broader point about democracy. Before the Great Die-Off our democracies were thoroughly imperfect, but they held within their institutions and cultures the prospect, the seeds, of their own refinement and improvement. This is the most striking and uplifting feature of democracy: it was an ongoing experiment that by design was an evolving project, something that was never settled, something that had to be achieved each and every generation and never taken for granted. Just as the existentialists argued that each human life is what one makes of it and nothing else, so too with democratic societies: we are free to change our societies through deliberation and collective action. If one does not like the direction society is going, then democracies not only permit but encourage civic engagement with the democratic processes and mechanisms that make change possible without violence. I know this very well because I lived this truth; I am this truth; this evening, *we are* this truth.

I will never deny the fact that the market democracies in the industrial age developed in ways that were environmentally devastating, to say nothing of their range of deep injustices and inequalities. Human societies will always be flawed and imperfect because we are flawed and imperfect. But by and large people in past democratic societies were free to speak their minds; to organise in their communities; to run for office; engage their representatives; to prefigure alternative cultures and vote politicians in and out of power. And as one reflects over the history of democratic societies one sees that these mechanisms, thoroughly imperfect though they were, steadily produced changes within those societies that can only be described as progressive; as a slow march toward a more justifiable social order.

Remember, for example, the remarkable achievements of the movements for women's rights, civil rights, and gay rights, to name only a few. Abolishing slavery; decolonising a nation; getting the vote; being free to marry whomever you loved without prejudice; removing the scar of racial segregation from society; being recognised as an equal before the law. Often these deep changes were unimaginable to the oppressed before their liberation—it all seemed too difficult, too entrenched, impossible to transcend—until one day, after years of struggle, a weakness or tipping point presented itself and people would wake up and find that the world had changed. That is what social movements do: they surprise us. And that element of surprise is what keeps the spark of hope alive. While utopia was certainly never achieved in any of the democratic societies, life for millions upon millions of people was dramatically improved through the mechanisms of democratic government and due process, as people demanded changes to the cultures and institutions of society.

None of these cultural and institutional changes came easy. They all came slower than was desirable and few if any were completely satisfactory in their effects and outcomes. But that just meant the call of civil engagement was not yet complete. It did not give anyone the right to throw democracy out the door and start blowing things up or killing people, like spoilt children who did not have the maturity to wield the power in their hands. No, the work of democracy is never done, because the promise of democracy is true. That is to say, we, homo sapiens, have the capacity as intelligent social animals to improve ourselves, to refine our institutions, to correct our errors, to protect the weak from the abuses of power, to expand our spheres of compassion, and to resolve our disputes without resort to violence.

This is what democracy means—what we are trying to create and practise today—but those are the mechanisms of change that Senjen and his team of murderers took from us by releasing Hemlock-42. However deeply flawed industrial civilisation was, and I was as fierce a critic as any, by virtue of its democratic constitution it had the potential to change or be changed; to transform fundamentally, and thus resolve its ecological contradictions in ways that did not require mass murder. But that possibility was taken from us through the unilateral action of a few mad scientists—a few megalomaniacs— who thought they had the right to decide the fate of our species. The arrogance of such action is simply indigestible. Even as I speak these words a nausea forms in my gut, thinking of what they did and the methods they chose to do it.

Given the democratic foundations of industrial society, how might we have resolved our ecological contradictions without resort to violence and mass murder? First of all, there was a communications task that needed to be met. By the turn of the 21st century the scientific evidence exposing our unsustainable impacts on Earth was convincing, and yet more work was needed communicating these insights in culturally sophisticated ways. It is not just what one says, but how one says it, that matters. Regrettably, the environmental movement was slow to appreciate this critical insight. But things were developing. The internet provided an almost free tool for mass distribution of information. An ecological consciousness was on the rise.

If more people had seen and felt the extent of ecological overshoot it would have been clear, even from a self-interested perspective, that one cannot have a healthy economy without a healthy ecosystem.

We would have changed for our own sakes; we would not have needed to be saints. But, just as importantly, it had become clear to growing portions of affluent societies that consumerism represented a false conception of human flourishing, even on its own terms. People were richer than ever in material terms and yet these high-impact consumers often lacked a sense of meaning and purpose in life; everyone seemed 'time poor' and always agitated; people were alienated from their communities and disconnected from natural systems. Something, sometime, had gone terribly wrong. Many people had achieved their dreams of material prosperity only to discover the dream was a nightmare. People knew this in their heads and felt it in their hearts.

What this meant was that there was a powerful counterculture developing beneath the surface of industrial society, waiting to explode. An awakening was underway. When people are dissatisfied with life, they seek an alternative, and a range of movements were emerging based on notions of 'simple living', minimalism, sufficiency, permaculture, and ecovillages. The fascinating thing about these movements was that they promised a triple dividend—that is, by reducing consumption, first, they lessened their environmental impacts, second, they left more for others in greater need, and third, the real attraction lay in the fact that they held up an alternative and more genuine conception of wellbeing. By exchanging superfluous consumption for more free time, more freedom, these countercultures were learning how to live more on less. They spoke of 'frugal abundance' and 'prosperous descent'. In short, the oppositional movements were discovering that they had been sold a lie by the marketers and advertisers; that one could not purchase happiness and that the good things in life really were free. As an ancient philosopher once wrote, 'He who knows he has enough is rich'—from which we can infer that those who have enough, but who do not know it, are poor.

This may all sound rather obvious to us today—of course nice clothes and fancy cars will not satisfy the human craving for meaning—but in the age of consumerism these were radical ideas that were struggling to break through the crust of mainstream culture. Admittedly, the simple living movements were insufficiently radical, poorly organised, and often politically naïve. But the same could be said of any social movement in its infancy. From little things big things grow.

What is more, imagining a powerful and organised 'simple living' movement was no more implausible than imagining powerful and organised women's rights, civil rights, or gay rights movements. Before they happened, it all seemed impossible; and then the impossible happened. As I have said, social movements surprise us, and only those people with small imaginations could not see the transformative potential in the range of countercultural environmental and social justice movements which, in the early decades of the 21st century, had yet to achieve maturity as political forces. Everywhere cracks were appearing in global capitalism. At any moment the floodgates of positive change could have burst asunder.

The key political point returns us to the matter of democracy. As subcultures began to reject consumerism and affluence and explore alternative low-impact material cultures of sufficiency, two things were bound to happen and were beginning to happen. First, those subcultures would have blurred into the dominant culture, as more people began to see that a 'simpler way' was a better and more satisfying way than the emptiness of affluence. But second, and even more importantly, as this profound cultural shift gained momentum these post-materialist cultural values inevitably would have come to inform and reshape political structures and economic systems and goals. A culture of people living lives of sufficiency would not accept a violent economic system that chews up rainforests and poisons rivers. Politicians would have seen that in order to maintain or achieve political power they would need to satisfy the voting public. A radical and organised counterculture could soon transform the deluded economics of growth into a viable economics of sufficiency. I will not argue that this would have been easy or even that it would have been likely. But it was a real possibility.

That possibility, however, was destroyed when Senjen released Hemlock-42. This act of violence went against every principle of democracy—it was the worst kind of vigilantism. To be clear, I am not arguing against resistance to immoral law. We all know that there is no necessary relationship between what is law and what is just. But the way we resist must have some values and our activism should prefigure the kind of world we are striving for. If our resistance is violent and dictatorial, we risk sparking a cycle of revenge. In fact, one of my biggest concerns for our new world is that our origin story is grounded in genocide. And once the unthinkable becomes history, the potential for it being repeated again in the future is much greater.

By contrast, when we resist in a non-violent and democratic way, we hold out the possibility of a better future. Only non-violent resistance affirms our common humanity and the idea that all human beings are capable of reform and redemption. Non-violent disobedience is a politics where the worth of each person is made essential. Imagine how much brighter our future would be if we could sit here now and tell our young people about the glorious transformation we wrought through non-violent struggle. Imagine how proud we would feel to tell that story. Instead we have the story of a Great Genocide.

To shift focus somewhat, there was also a deep uncertainty about the future that Senjen refused to acknowledge—and it is an uncertainty that fundamentally undermines his violent strategy even further. Sure, the scientific evidence was mounting that industrial civilisation was undermining planetary ecosystems in dangerous ways. Sure, the prospect of cultural enlightenment or political leadership may not have inspired anyone with confidence that the problems we were facing would or could be solved. But the arc of time is not a straight line; its course proceeds through twists and turns, and this means one is deceived if one imagines a future that is merely an extension of the present.

The point is that even if all the evidence justified a tragic pessimism about the human situation on Earth, one could retain a sense of grounded hope merely by virtue of the unknowability of the future. Eco-systemic collapse may have been likely but it was not a certainty; the dynamics of climate change may not have played out quite as badly as the scientists forewarned; an unforeseen (and unforeseeable) social movement may have arisen out of nowhere and institutionalised the rights of nature just as previous eras had institutionalised the right to vote or free speech. As I've just discussed, at the time of the Great Die-Off, a thousand social movements were bubbling under the surface of culture, waiting for their opportunity to burst into the mainstream. In short, any number of black swans could have been around the next bend in the river, set to change things for the better; to buy us more time; to cast humanity off onto a new, less destructive path.

As I have said, it was only a limited imagination that closed these possibilities off to Senjen. If he had acknowledged the infinite variables that shape the unfolding of life on Earth, his brash confidence in his own assessment of the future would have dissolved into humility. He would have seen the deep uncertainties in the path of humankind, and in conditions of uncertainty one must take appropriate precautions before jumping to radical conclusions. For instance, if you have encountered a certain snake whose poison is fatal, you would want to be sure you have been bitten before you cut your arm off to stop the poison's flow to your heart. If you are unsure, or if alternatives to amputation exist, show the wisdom to hesitate! All the more so if it is someone else's arm!

We could see this line of reasoning as a form of the precautionary principle: If the consequences of your intervention are irreversible and will bring great suffering, be sure the intervention is absolutely necessary. Show great caution before engaging in such drastic interventions, and the more drastic the consequences of the intervention, the more caution that should be shown. It seems to me that Senjen and his collaborators showed insufficient caution—to the point of criminality. The extremity of their action—mass murder of innocents to protect nature—demanded a confidence in its necessity that simply did not exist. And even if it did exist, there are some means that no end can justify. This is clearly such a case.

Let me make one final point. There is also a simple utilitarian calculus that provides further grounds for rejecting any defence that Senjen and his collaborators could offer. Their acts led to the appalling suffering of more than seven billion people, most of whom died painfully, suffering not only the physical pain brought on by the virus but, perhaps even more significantly, the incalculable emotional anguish of seeing their loved ones die in their arms, undignified, like lab rats that Senjen had decided were no longer useful. If the morality of an act is determined by whether it produces more happiness than pain in aggregate, then hands down releasing Hemlock-42 was an immoral act, since billions suffered while today a small fraction of that number live comfortable lives. Releasing Hemlock-42 caused far more suffering than it saved or avoided. As if there were not enough to condemn them already, this calculus adds further weight to the prosecution's compelling case. Even on its own it would suffice in producing a guilty verdict.

In closing, let me speak briefly to the question of how the sole surviving perpetrator should be held accountable, should a consensus form that he is guilty of crimes against humanity. Immanuel Wright, our first prosecutor, called for a sentence of death, and one can understand and even sympathise with the flow of his logic. If Durruk Senjen was prepared to destroy the lives of billions, then in retribution the gift of life should be taken from him.

But, of course, the simplicity of this logic can be deceiving, tempting though it is to cast the guilty into the fire. No doubt there would be a certain perverse satisfaction that flowed from hearing Senjen scream. It may come as no surprise, however, that the logic of my own analysis demands a very different approach. Just as I object to the violence they enacted on so many, so too do I feel we would be reducing ourselves to their level if we answered their violence with our own. We have no more right to take his life as they had the right to murder billions. Let him live, I implore you, but insist that he lives in exile and dies in exile. We should not have to be reminded that we are of the same species.

May the Great Spirit have mercy on their souls.

Having said her piece, Mohandria Bentharma hobbles back into the mass of tribespeople and disappears. There seems to be very mixed feelings as the crowd begins to digest and discuss Aunty's speech, but the integrity of her words evokes a universal civility, such that even those in furious disagreement remain calm and committed to the process of peaceful discourse. Again, Zola Eblo is seen walking amongst the crowd collecting scattered wood for the fire. After dumping another armful of fuel in a growing pile at her feet, she invites a representative of the Youth Council to speak.

6. THE LESSER EVIL

Andrea Lorde, known to her friends as Greenshoot, is from the first generation of children born after the Great Die-Off. She is a tall woman with flowing auburn hair and tanned skin from the hours she spends in the sun. Head gardener in her community, she has spent years rediscovering techniques for companion planting and natural weed control, as well as designing and establishing her community's largest food forest. She is popular amongst the younger generation gathered at the ceremony and she was recently elected as the lead spokesperson for a fledging Youth Council which was established to represent young people in the surviving communities. The young look to her as a voice and she can feel their eyes on her, encouraging her to stand and speak.

In recent years, a divide has emerged between those who survived the Great Die-off and the first generation born in the new society. Intergenerational conflict is not new but this one has an edge to it. Whether hard feelings are the product of survivors' guilt or a sense of betrayal, nobody can tell. Whatever the case, things have been left to fester and this gathering is the first invitation the Youth Council has received to speak openly and honestly about the past and the world they have inherited.

As Andrea walks to the front of the crowd, many of the older generation stiffen, holding their middle as though bracing for impact. But they cannot see any malice in Andrea's face as she stands in front of the crowd. Andrea waits until Mohandria has resumed her seat before speaking.

Brothers and sisters; aunties and uncles. I am honoured to be the first young person to speak before you today. From our oral histories and from the access we have to old books, I have learned that past societies failed to listen to the young and dismissed their pleas as emotional and immature; naïve and idealistic. Some of us, on occasion, were given platforms. We were permitted to address world leaders and captains of industry, but rarely were our ideas taken on board or acted on. Toward the end of the 'petroleum interval' young people went on strike—refusing to go to school. They deschooled themselves, that is, in order to be better citizens in the midst of an unfolding climate emergency. And many withdrew their participation in a system that was really only training them to be obedient workers in an economy that cared not for their future. I am yet to be convinced that human beings have the capacity to learn from history—but I do hope that we don't make those mistakes again.

With respect, I was surprised to hear Aunty Bentharma speak so hopefully about democracy in the Age of Empire. I did not live in the Before Time, but since I was young, you adults have told us constantly that we are building something different now—something 'truly democratic'. A politics where people get an actual say in decisions that impact their lives. The democracy we are building here goes beyond elections and the opportunity to respond to predetermined questions or predictable response mechanisms. In our emergent Youth Council, we have been learning skills for active listening, consensus decision-making, and how to feed our ideas and decisions into the other councils. Right now, I am the lead spokesperson for the youth—but another person will replace me in a year. And so the wheel will keep turning and new ideas and voices will be heard. That is as it should be.

What we are trying to build here is a negation of the structures we once had. Our council structure gives voice to all people—the youth, women, men, and the elderly. We even nominate people to represent and defend the interests of other species and ecosystems. Spokespeople from each council meet twice a month to debate, deliberate, and make decisions about things that impact our lives. Positions are vacated every year and new representatives are chosen so that power does not become entrenched and new ideas and energy are captured. We have been taught from birth that all people have intelligence and that politics is a responsibility we share for the good of the whole. Yes, we have some representative roles, but our primary commitment is to participatory democracy, where we all practise, and are expected to practise, self-governance. We also have made provision for extraordinary meetings like this one, where everyone has a say and can listen to our deliberations. This is what democracy looks like.

How many of you have said that we are going to do things properly this time? That we are striving for a truer version of democracy? But if what we had in the Before Time worked sufficiently well—as Aunty seemed to suggest—why aren't we just rebuilding those lost structures and systems of governance? If what we had before was adequate, why do so many of you teach us about the dangers of career politicians, the influence of money on politics, or the 'Plutocratic era', when those who guarded their wealth like dragons were elected to positions of power and ran the state like a corporation. If Aunty thinks past democracies were going to deal with climate change, why do we talk about the 'hollowing'—when people abandoned associations and became dissociated from politics. It was an era of surveillance capitalism, in which elections were being managed by private firms and the tech giants were shaping public consciousness through their politicised messaging. From where was an ecologically sensitive and democratically minded multitude going to emerge?

Aunty spoke about public debate and described an ideal speech situation where reason prevailed over self-destruction. But we know from our own experiences that we are not rational animals and that reason is a slave to our passions. And it is no use pretending now—after we have lost everything—that rationality could prevail in a climate where global powers were pushing denial and self-interest, and delaying action. Where is the evidence that suggests that evidence was enough? Even the examples Aunty gave us were partial and limited at best.

I have only learned about the civil rights movement in old books and through lessons in oral history. But is Aunty suggesting that the movement liberated African Americans from the powers of racism that coursed through society? It would be a great relief to me if that were true. But if civil rights challenged racism, why were African Americans still demanding that 'Black Lives Matter' in the years before the Great Die-Off? Why did the prison system reproduce slavery—even forcing inmates to manufacture cheap products for giant corporations? These are the achievements of your version of democracy. And if your democracies could not radically challenge something like racism, why should we have confidence that it would make a dent in arguably even more complicated global problems like climate change, resource depletion, and poverty?

As you can tell, I am deeply troubled by the dissonance between Aunty's speech and what we have been taught. I can only conclude that either some of you are influenced by nostalgia or our education is deficient. I hope it is the latter because that would give me some confidence that what we are trying to build here is truly based on learnings from the past.

On other matters, I feel that I can speak with more confidence and certainty. At each of the meetings of our Youth Council we have been almost unanimous in affirming the actions of Senjen and his colleagues. You may think that this is because we did not live through the Great Die-Off and did not see our loved ones die. That much is true. But we prioritise a different truth: if not for their actions, we would not be alive. Period. Older generations were not fulfilling their most basic responsibility—which was to secure the conditions of life for future generations. So Senjen and his team intervened—in a drastic but necessary way. They were the only ones who really fought for future generations.

If we are to advance this discussion today, I need you to make a space in your minds for a grey area—between good and evil, perhaps even *beyond* good and evil. Life presents itself in technicolour and rarely offers us simple choices. How many of us here have had to make a decision that has hurt someone? Faced with a hard choice we cannot just throw our hands in the air and refuse to make a judgement—that itself would be a decision. And one that consecrates the status quo. The responsible thing to do is try to calculate the *least bad option*. That is what those scientists did. The only difference between their choice and our everyday judgements is *scale*. To think otherwise is to suggest that hard choices cease or must be abandoned when the stakes get high. And that is not a position that the youth can accept.

On this issue of determining 'the least bad option' I must also respond to the critique Aunty Bentharma presented based on what she called the 'utilitarian calculus'. She argued that the suffering caused by the Great Die-Off outweighed any good that flowed from it, and thus was immoral. With respect, it seems she lacked perspective, such that her calculus didn't count everything it should have. No one will deny that the Great Die-Off caused great suffering, but let us also acknowledge that it avoided great suffering and created the conditions for incalculable wellbeing. Billions in the Before Time suffered in conditions of destitution, while a minority lived agitated and hollow lives in pursuit of luxury and social status. And who dares to calculate the suffering of our fellow animals—the cows, pigs, and chickens who were being industrially farmed in conditions of unspeakable cruelty, only to be slaughtered by the tens of billions every year?

On balance, then, it seems clear that most people and most animals suffered more than they thrived. Furthermore, industrial civilisation, in its historically short existence, was in the process of undermining the ecological conditions for wellbeing—not just human wellbeing but the wellbeing of the entire community of life. Extinction was on the cards. How does one account for all this in the utilitarian calculus? By releasing Hemlock-42 and rebalancing the human economy and population on Earth, the community of life now has an opportunity to flourish into the deep future—for millions and millions of years—provided we learn from history. If we account for that in the utilitarian calculus, the good derived from the release of Hemlock-42 clearly outweighs the admittedly horrid, but nevertheless short term, suffering caused to humanity. It may seem like an evil act, but it was the lesser evil, and thus no evil at all. This is especially so since the suffering caused was likely to have come anyway, probably in greater waves, as Empire was destined for a catastrophic collapse. And so, it is quite clear that the utilitarian perspective leads not to an indictment but to a defence of Senjen and his colleagues.

In much the same way, I can easily deconstruct Aunty Bentharma's distorted interpretation of the precautionary principle. She argued that if the consequences of one's actions are irreversible and will bring great suffering, one must be sure the intervention is necessary. With some justification, she argued that one must show great caution before engaging in such drastic interventions, and the more drastic the consequences of the intervention, the more caution that should be shown. This is indeed sound logic, and it suggests a preliminary case against the release of Hemlock-42. But it is not determinative and ultimately, I will suggest, it is supportive of precisely the opposite conclusion than that which Aunty Bentharma maintained. Basically, she was advocating that, in the spirit of precaution, people wait for the Apocalypse.

The example Aunty gave to support her case drew on the analogy of a snake bite. She said if you are unsure whether you have been bitten by a poisonous snake, show precaution before cutting off your arm to stop the poison's flow to your heart, especially if alternatives to amputation exist, and show even more precaution if it is someone else's arm. Again, her reasoning is sound so far as it goes. But what if you are almost certain that you or a loved one has indeed been bitten by the snake and that effective alternative remedies do not exist? In this case, one must take great precautions to ensure you or your loved one are not terminated by the poison. For the love of life: amputate! Amputate! It would not be precautious to wait. It would not be precautious to see whether some untested antidote happened to work. That would be reckless and irresponsible. One must be brave enough to act out of precaution, difficult though it may be, and intervene to stop the most likely outcome of the tragic situation. Industrial civilisation was bringing an end to the story of life. It is hard to imagine a greater loss in this infinite and empty universe. Accordingly, the precautionary principle dictates that drastic action was justified to prevent this incalculable loss. Again, clear moral reasoning is on the side of Senjen, even if this contradicts superficial moral intuitions.

Rather than engage with this logic, Aunty writes off Senjen as acting merely out of adolescent rage. With respect, at this point Aunty was degenerating into polemics that were bordering on defamation. Why are some of you so afraid of trying to see things from Senjen's perspective? You may not agree with his explanation, but he has no reason to lie. Think about it this way: if someone violently invades your home you should not stay calm and invite them in for a cup of tea. You do not try to reason with them as they are beating your child. No, you do what you need to do to protect yourself and those you care about from the criminal activity.

The same logic applies on a larger scale. You were living in a world where 90% of the large fish were gone, there was ten times as much plastic as plankton in the ocean, 77% of forests had been destroyed, 98% of grasslands were gone, species were collapsing and there was dioxin in every mother's breast milk. At what point were you going to fight back? Why were most of you so unwilling to draw a line in the sand? It is no good pontificating about sustainable consumption or dogmatic principles of non-violence if you could not achieve your stated goals of ecological viability. As an activist in the Before Time said: 'Non-violence is not a moral principle but a strategy: there is no moral goodness in using an ineffective weapon.' We needed effective deeds, not empty words or symbolic gestures.

Our oral histories talk a lot of your worries about how future generations would judge you. Well the Youth Council has had that conversation and we find you wanting. We are at a loss to understand how you could be shepherded so far down the path to extinction—like sheep to the slaughter.

The Youth Council agrees that Senjen and his colleagues were acting in self-defence. They did not introduce violence. They were responding to the Sixth Mass Extinction; responding to a time when human greed risked destroying 95% of life on Earth. It would take incredible arrogance to claim that the human lives lost during the Great Die-Off were of more value than the 121 million pigs that were killed each day for food in the United States or the hundreds of species that were going extinct every year. We know with certainty that emotions like laughter and empathy can be found in other animals. I have seen the intelligence in the eyes of our fellow animal creatures with whom we share this planet. The dogs in our community display feelings of guilt and have a sense of fairness that is barely distinguishable from our own. I recall reading about a study where a chimpanzee refused to accept food rewards until its friends and family were given some too. Animals are not as selfish as people once assumed. And their murder was taking place at a rate that—if we were being morally honest—puts the discussion before us today in a much more sobering context.

Let me ask you a different question. How many of you sincerely thought that industrial society was going to undergo a voluntary transition to a sane and sustainable way of living? When I ask this question of my elders, almost always I am told that the chances of such a transformation were slim to non-existent. And where were your models for genuine sustainability? Industrial society was unsustainable. It destroys the land-base and ecosystems upon which it relies. Can you provide a single example of a human settlement in industrial society—even a so-called 'eco-village'—that lived in a truly sustainable way? In a way that could be globalised to the whole population? I have asked that question countless times and have never received a satisfying answer. It seems everyone knew that things were going to hell and that conventional means of resistance were failing and destined to fail. On that basis: what ought to have been done?

We have been listening to your stories for decades now. It seems to me that you were all under some collective delusion that individual action was going to save the world. That if you retrofitted your houses, took shorter showers, and kept a vegetable garden, you could avoid catastrophe. I don't mean to be glib or misrepresent your history. But it is impossible for us young people to understand the radical individualism of that time. If I am honest, most of it sounds to us like a light-green fantasy intended to mitigate middle-class guilt. The master's tools were never going to bring down the master's house.

Why didn't you stand up for yourselves and withdraw your labour from the economy? Why didn't you blockade each site where a new coal plant was going to be built? Hell, why didn't you seize power and put each of those politicians who had been bought off by the fossil fuel industry up against the wall? It has been done before and what did you have to lose? Your silence was not going to save you! And it certainly wasn't going to save us, of the next generation!

Let me pull back a bit. I have fallen into simplistic judgements—the very thing I was just chastising others for. It is not my intention to open old wounds or cast blame. I know that some of you here did resist and I don't want to inflame tensions further in our community. I have also read about the economic dependency trap wherein it became difficult to move away from capitalism, since getting secure employment was what was needed to survive in a society dominated by capitalist processes. I know that capitalism beat you down and sucked your life-energy like a vampire. No wonder so many sought refuge in the hollow distractions of alcohol, drugs, and television.

Our real enemies are those who set us on the path of destruction and the capitalist system that coerced people into pursuing never-ending growth on a finite planet. Some writers in the past thought that capitalism's environmental impact was so significant that it was going to crash and be replaced with a more sustainable economic structure. But what they didn't seem to grasp was capitalism's power to internalise crisis and rebuild in a stronger form. Your history provides countless examples where capitalism did not shrink back from destroying people, communities, and even whole indigenous populations. In the end, it was going to claim us all. Deaths from starvation and habitat destruction were never going to unravel capitalism, precisely because most of the world's population had already become redundant. You were already disposable.

Not even your governments had the power to liberate people or challenge capitalism. In fact, it seems that your governments thought that their primary responsibility was to facilitate growth. I am not sure how you distinguished your politicians from business leaders. They parroted the same economic arguments and moved seamlessly between sectors as through a revolving door. In time many companies controlled more wealth than nation states—but by that time most of the damage had already been done.

I understand the impulse to hold somebody responsible for a tragedy. But I urge you to turn your attention to economics, not Senjen and his colleagues. Capitalism had its own perverted logic and coercive laws which bound many of you to its service. Like a multi-headed hydra, it was powerful and could not be defeated by severing a single head. It also seemed to rob you of the imagination to comprehend a life outside of its grasp. We understand that but urge you not to compound your past mistakes by making another one here today. To the youth, your judgement of Senjen sounds like a denial of our existence. The only reason we exist is because of his act of self-defence.

For that bravery, we express our gratitude.

As Andrea makes her way back to her seat there are some uncomfortable stirrings from within the crowd. Some of those gathered are visibly upset and call out to express their feelings. One of the attendees picks up a stick and hurls it toward Andrea in anger, but it misses and comes to rest near the fire. Andrea does not acknowledge the outburst and sits back down alongside other members of the Youth Council. Her resolve is firm but the atmosphere is as tense as it has been and the elders begin to wonder if the proceedings might soon break up.

7. Technofix

Zola gets to her feet and raises a hand in the air—a gesture for silence.

My friends. Let us not pollute this sacred space with these outbursts. We all knew before our Dadirri ceremony began that we would hear things that upset and challenge us. We knew that we would be tested. That is why we created a sacred space and called to our side those elements that speak of calm, patient reflection. Let us take a moment to sit in silence and think about what we have heard so far. We are not through yet—not by a long shot. And we are sure to hear more things that push us and rouse old feelings of hurt and anguish. Let us sit with that pain. Do not try to push it away.

Silence returns to the multitude and as thoughts press on old wounds, tears and moans are heard from different corners of the gathering. Zola waits for the outpouring to settle before continuing.

My friends. Let us recommit to Dadirri. Let us listen deeply and with a vulnerability that allows space for a new idea to take root or for an old idea to be softened. Let our words act like a plough for loosening the soil of contemplative thought. As you know, we have no rules for how to proceed from here, but I would like to call upon one of our number, Isaac Smith. I saw you just now throw something at our young friend. In the spirit of reconciliation, perhaps you would like to use this opportunity to stand up here and share your thoughts?

Isaac shifts uncomfortably in his seat—his face reddening with embarrassment. Just for a moment an image flashes before Zola's eyes—Maccari's famous work, Cicero Denounces Catiline. She does not linger on the thought. Like so many other pieces of art, the painting is no doubt long destroyed or lost.

Eventually Isaac stands and makes his way to the front of the crowd, acknowledging Zola as she returns to her space near the fire. Isaac speaks.

Friends. I wish to begin by apologising to Andrea. I am embarrassed by my impulsive actions and ask for your forgiveness. It is hard for those of us who lived in the Before Time to listen to your judgements. I thought that I had buried the pain of the past and pushed away my feelings of grief. But this space has brought the past rushing back. For the first time in many years, I can clearly see the faces of my children and loved ones—it's as though they are right here with us, although their faces have not aged in my mind. I am also restimulated by Andrea's anti-capitalist rhetoric, which I can only assume is based on a lack of historical understanding. If only you could better appreciate, Andrea, what happened in the 20th century when people tried to destroy the system and build a new utopia upon entirely new foundations. What a naïve and dangerous lack of historical understanding you and your supporters show. I had hoped we could leave all that behind—but it seems I was wrong. Many of those old books survive and I have no wish to suppress ideas, even those I think are wrongheaded and which have been disproven.

I was also one of those of whom Andrea spoke that struggled to convince governments and companies to act on climate change. The young today cannot comprehend how hard we worked or the toll it took on our health and personal lives. And I fought not only against climate denialists but also against those irrational factions of the environmental movement who refused to be guided by science, rationality, and the power of markets to shape and incentivise human behaviour for the good. If we defenders of the free market had a failing—visible with the benefit of hindsight—it was our failure to analyse desire and instead to too often take it as given. Admittedly, my fellow economists and I were slow to learn of the various mindfulness practices that offer different perspectives on the nature of desire and how it arises; how desire can be re-contextualised in one's mental universe so that we spend less time in compulsive consumption and more time in alternative approaches to living that offer more reward and security. But even when reflecting on the need in the Before Time to reshape human desire away from shallow consumerism, it is clear that ultimately this was a marketing challenge. We needed to revalue what was valued. So if marketing was the poison, I contend it was also the cure.

In any case, my perspective on the past is somewhat different from those who have already spoken. I think it is uncontroversial that Senjen and his colleagues committed premeditated murder. It was radical evil, as Immanuel Wright said. Even here in this place, we have not strayed so far from civilisation to regard the murder of innocents as anything but murder. And had civilisation survived they would have been tried, convicted, and punished. Andrea and others can contort themselves in any way they wish, but nothing they say can change these simple facts.

But we don't live in that world anymore. We have no states, courts, or independent judges. We don't have a legal system and have made no social contract to be bound by the norms that govern us now. Perhaps in time we will get back to something like we had in the Before Time—the Rule of Law—but we are not there yet. We have no jurisdiction to prosecute or punish. And so, I see this gathering as having a cathartic and therapeutic, rather than a juridical, function.

In contrast with Mohandria Bentharma, I am skeptical about democracy. Many of you have heard me talk about this before—surely you can see that it is only one way to govern? And our history illustrates that there are great risks in allowing everyone a say in decision making. Far better to be led by those with the knowledge and expertise to make decisions on behalf of everyone else. Not philosopher kings but a political class that has developed the skills for governing. What we have now might work while we are small, but we will want more centralisation as we grow and expand over a larger area.

To my mind, democracy was one of the greatest obstacles to change. We had the technology to power the world and lift the poor from poverty. We were also working on ventures that could suck carbon from the atmosphere, make clouds more reflective, and fertilise the oceans to grow plankton. But at every turn we were resisted by those who allowed emotion and fear to determine their thinking. As a species, we were incredibly skilled at using tools to live in the world. And yet, each time we proposed a technical solution to the climate crisis we were met with jeers and accused of meddling with the balance of nature. It was almost as though people did not really understand what it meant to live in the Anthropocene. We were not gods, but none could deny that our powers had become god-like. Our task was to make the Anthropocene good, for the power was in our hands.

For years environmentalists declared that we were living in the Anthropocene era. The Union of Geological Sciences made it official in 2024, but what did that mean? If we could focus on the science for just a moment, the upshot was that human beings had become a geological force. That our actions were altering the *earth system as a whole*. If you stop and think about this for a moment that means that there is no such thing as pristine nature or wilderness that can be separated from human beings. There was no nature 'out there'. The Anthropocene literally meant that human beings had become the weather makers. This is a fundamentally anthropocentric idea that recognised that humans were unique and different from other animals.

That might not be an ideal situation—in fact you might describe the emergence of the Anthropocene as the greatest tragedy in human history. But once we were in the Anthropocene there was no use pretending that we could just withdraw back from nature and let it evolve without us. The only interesting question was: how should we respond? How would we choose to exercise the responsibilities that came with our new-found power? To my mind this required an enlightened anthropocentrism that balanced power and responsibility.

My experience also taught me to be cautious of proposals that promoted a radical break with the present. However desirable it might have been for people to consume less, transition toward a 'new system', and combat global poverty using green-tech, that was *never* going to happen within the time period we had to respond. I did not see a single serious proposal that contradicted that fact. And while some people chastised me for lacking imagination, I was just being logical and practical. Neither optimistic nor pessimistic, but realistic. My criteria for change were very simple—understand that most people did not want to change their lives and that the majority of the world's people wanted to be lifted from poverty; and refuse all proposals that are impractical or would not make an impact. In short—*realpolitik* not utopianism.

There is no better example of our refusal to be guided by science and logic than past battles over nuclear power. I had no love for the technology or the corporations that ran roughshod over local laws to get their way. I knew very well of the Chernobyl disaster, where Soviet incompetence killed thirty-one people and thousands more from cancer. However, in subsequent disasters very few were killed or even harmed. My understanding is that the accident on Three Mile Island was not major. And the meltdown at Fukushima, far from turning me away from nuclear, turned me into an advocate, since again the damage was regrettable but not extensive. Public anxiety over nuclear energy was not based on evidence but produced mainly from fear mongering by environmentalists.

As I look around, I can see surprise on some of your faces. Does what I say surprise you? Think about things rationally. In Fukushima an old plant was hit by a gigantic earthquake and a tsunami and yet only *one* person was killed from radiation. That gave me confidence that we were improving and gradually perfecting the technology and that most of the resistance to nuclear power was based on misinformation.

But how did the Green groups respond? Only climate deniers or anti-vaxxers exhibited a similar disregard for science and dealt in so many lies. In the wake of Fukushima there grew a global campaign to decommission or not replace nuclear plants. Where did those activists think the gap in energy was going to come from? We don't need to guess. The cost of renewables was still high when Hemlock-42 was released and they had limited capacity to replace the constant flow of electricity from dispatchable energy sources like coal or nuclear. And we had no batteries that could affordably supply power to cities for days.

Retrofitting utilities to renewable energy was an engineering nightmare. For most economies, the transition was going to cost more than years of GDP. The best scientific and economic analyses indicated that billions spent on renewable energy technologies would only reduce dependence on fossil fuels by a fraction, especially as energy demand kept growing. Contrast this to a country like France, which was able to transition to nuclear power and substantially decarbonise their electricity grid in just fifteen years! We could have got that time down dramatically once processes for standardisation and repetition in production were in place.

Countries like England and Germany did eventually move away from nuclear power, but they met their energy needs with a combination of coal and shale gas. I don't need to spell out the impact that this had on carbon emissions and many of you would have heard my mantra: 'Coal kills more people when it goes right than nuclear power does when it goes wrong.' Nuclear power was the safest kind of energy we had ever created. This is particularly true when compared against mining accidents, hydroelectric dam failures, gas explosions, and all the accidents caused from transporting fossil fuels.

I never understood how environmentalists could champion climate research but turn their back on science when its conclusions did not fit their prejudices and biases. Of course, some did understand, and I admit that the issue of nuclear waste was always something that troubled me. But given the urgency, I was willing to live with my misgivings. A technical problem ought not have stood in the way of us taking radical steps to reduce emissions. And besides, human ingenuity was developing a new generation of nuclear plants that were compact and ran on waste! That waste would have been recycled until it was broken down and it had a half-life of mere decades. In a rational universe, those working on the integral fast reactors would have won the noble peace prize and their names would have been as well-known as Newton's and Einstein's. But as we know, they were never given the support to complete this great work.

Battle lines were also drawn over geoengineering. I was less convinced by this path. But as governments failed to take action, we were forced to look at radical solutions and I did not see the point of trying to tackle global warming without looking at the portfolio of available technologies. We needed to have all options on the table and investigate them with scientific rigour. There was no sense fighting global warming with one arm tied behind our backs.

One of my last projects as a scientist involved solar geoengineering which proposed injecting aerosols of tiny reflective particles into the highest reaches of the stratosphere. This technology could be released very quickly and relatively cheaply, and once in place, those particles would simulate the effect of a volcanic eruption and reflect sunlight back into space. Like any technology, there were dangers and risks, but I was confident that we could calculate and model the right dose of particles to release. When Hemlock-42 was released we had just finalised an international code of conduct and governance with the United Nations. Key principles in the agreement were that the public should be able to participate in decision-making, research would be published in open-access journals, and all impacts would go through independent assessment. My colleagues and I all thought that those rules were reasonable and would grant us a public license to continue our research.

Another technology I was working on was slow acting but had long-term potential. It involved engineering plants so that they could store more carbon in their root system. The idea was to focus on crops that we already planted on a large scale—such as wheat, soya beans, corn, and cotton. These crops would not only act as a carbon sink but—and this is the genius part—the extra carbon would increase productivity and so increase food production. Thus, these perfect plants would empower us to tackle climate change and address world hunger. This research was being funded by major agriculture companies and our test crops were showing great potential.

Most of the objections we received focused on the idea that we were playing God or altering nature. Once again this reflected a fundamental lack of understanding about the Anthropocene—human beings were already altering the Earth system as a whole. There was no such thing as pristine nature that existed apart from human beings. That was Holocene thinking and we could no sooner go back to that epoch than we could wish away our new-found power.

Others criticised us for taking money from technology and agriculture companies that sought to profit from research. This argument always assumed that my colleagues and I lacked the integrity to be independent and at arm's length from our funders. Moreover, my focus was primarily on the science—not on idealistic attempts to change every human structure that was in place. Once again, my position was that we needed to work within the structures and institutions that were in place and not try to reimagine our economic system while simultaneously tackling the greatest existential crisis that humankind had ever faced. Looking back we know all too well what happened when utopian thinkers in the 20th century demolished the existing institutions and systems and attempted to build an entirely new society based on new ideals. The result was a gang of murderers taking over the state. The result was National Socialism and the Gulags.

Besides, my dispassionate opinion is that capitalism, markets, and price systems were the best way to govern selfish-human behaviour. Experts in ethnology and evolutionary biology had identified the will to self-preservation or the 'selfish gene' as an integral aspect of the human condition. Of course, we are not determined by our genes, and of course there is evidence of human cooperation, but there is no use denying this material aspect of our nature or thinking that we can create ideal utopias based on abstract ideas and naïve hopes for human altruism. I won't bore you now with the litany of historical examples where societies came to ruin because a small group of people thought that complex social relations should be radically altered to pursue some abstract idea. Such endeavours will always lead to the tragic mismanagement of common resources and, as I said before, the imposition of a corrupt centralised bureaucracy ruled over by violent thugs and villains.

Ultimately, the most powerful moral objection to the release of Hemlock-42 was captured in the concise opening statement from Immanuel Wright. The release was a deliberate act, intended to kill billions, which violated human rights to life. It really is that simple. But the Great Die-Off becomes even more obscene when one recognises that it was not only wrong but unnecessary, which is the contribution I have been trying to make. In short, my position is that we didn't need to murder billions of innocent people. We had the technology and the market mechanisms capable of solving climate change and which could simultaneously improve the human condition through ongoing economic growth. We didn't need to overthrow capitalism—whatever that meant. We just needed to practise and regulate it better and in a more humane way. We also needed structures that could manage selfish human instincts and incentivise behaviour that would advance the common good.

Which brings me to the question before us today: what should we do with Professor Senjen, whose guilt is plain to see? As I said at the outset, we no longer live in a society of positive law and we have no agreed upon process for administering norms. It would also be unjust for us to formulate a law now and apply that retrospectively on their actions. In this time of lawlessness, we can only be guided by dispassionate reason and logic. Central to our thinking should be two basic ideas—proportionality and the need to disincentivise anybody from doing something similar in the future.

I have been thinking a lot about this and I want you to reflect on my suggestion for some time before responding to it. First, I want to be clear that I don't think the perpetrator can be punished, as such, for his actions. Punishment presumes that people can be reconciled, and it leaves open the possibility that those involved can cohabit the world in the future. But there are some extreme acts where people break the bonds of sociality that are inherent to the human condition and place themselves beyond the reach of forgiveness. In this instance, I also question whether we survivors can forgive on behalf of those that died. Christ had a way out of such a bind when he said that it would be better for such people to have a large millstone hung around their neck and to be drowned in the depths of the sea. But I also oppose the death penalty on the grounds that we, who have known so much death, are numb to its effect. Thus, it could not act as a deterrent.

What I propose is this—Senjen should have one eye gouged from his face. An eye for an eye. It is an act rich with symbolic meaning and its visibility will act as a reminder to anyone who even contemplates the ultimate crime—deciding with whom they wish to share the Earth. Senjen should also be exiled from all and any of our communities and forced to wander from settlement to settlement, begging for food and a place to rest. Let him wander without aim for the rest of his days with only his thoughts and perhaps his regrets for company. That way, if anybody thinks about doing such a thing again, they will picture Senjen's bloody face and recall the taunts that children will aim in his direction. The rocks thrown at his back. Only something as visceral as that can provide the deterrent. We need to live without fear that such cruelty will visit us again.

Isaac's proposal evokes a roar of approval from certain sections of the crowd, which immediately provokes an opposing array of boos and groans of disapproval amongst others. A heated argument erupts between two young men seated near each other, and soon people are required to intervene as their discourse collapses into aggressive pushing and shoving. Again, there are fears that the emotionally charged gathering could prove too much for civil discussion to be maintained, but the elders let the people vent. For a long time voices are raised as reactions are cast about in high passion, even as Senjen sits quietly and just stares into the fire with a certain severity. Eventually, however, the assembly settles down and people await the next speaker. Zola nods to someone in the shadows.

8. Anarcho-Primitivism

Jack Zanzer, a frail, austere old man, emerges from the darkness and moves stiffly toward the fire pit that is serving as a backdrop for the speakers. The blue-grey moonlight shines off his bald head and his long grey beard sways softly in the night's rising breeze. Jack's various physical ticks put his autism on display and those people closest to the fire pit see a terrifying depth in his eyes—at once profound and empty—no doubt owing to his life spent in voluntary solitude, an outcast philosopher content to spend his days devouring the spectacle of his own mind.

In the Before Time, Jack was a child prodigy of unfathomable brilliance. After leaving school at thirteen due to an intolerable boredom, he received a scholarship to write a PhD in the Faculty of Philosophy at Oxford University, which he completed in seven months, receiving first class honours. His thesis was simply called 'Anarcho-Primitivism: Civilisation for the Deep Future', which he self-published and proceeded to sell more than a million copies of in the first year, despite a rather self-aggrandising and somewhat contradictory retail price. Although he received offers for tenured professorships at Oxford, Cambridge, Harvard, and every one of the so-called ivy league universities, Jack declined them all on the grounds he had already said everything he had to say and therefore didn't want to spend his life re-writing his PhD, which, in his own words, was already 'perfectly clear and concise'. He disappeared from the global stage as quickly as he had entered.

With the generous proceeds from book sales Jack Zanzer purchased a large tract of land in the mountains of what was then Croatia, where he had intended to live out his life as a recluse, waiting for the End Times. And yet, somehow, this mysterious figure finds himself standing before the gathered audience this evening. Lacking any sense of social etiquette or conventions, he wastes no time with formalities and begins his substantive contribution rather abruptly, speaking in a steady monotone that nevertheless conveys, without arrogance, supreme confidence in the message being delivered.

There is only one way to live on this Earth without degrading people and without degrading the ecological health of the land-base, waterways, forests, and air upon which we all rely. That way of life is what I call anarcho-primitivism: a radically simple living, low-tech, primarily hunter-gatherer existence, without much agriculture and without a centralised governance system that we used to call 'the state'. To live otherwise is to initiate a civilisational sickness unto death.

I suspect you may not want to believe this. You may find it depressing, even unacceptable, that humanity must live within the physical, technological, and political boundaries of anarcho-primitivism. You may invent all types of ideologies, practices, and technologies that attempt to avoid this truth of existence. But I tell you now, by force of logic and evidence, any society that defies the fundamental precepts of anarcho-primitivism will begin walking the path toward inevitable collapse. With history as my witness! As consumption and production increase beyond the most basic material and technological needs; as agriculture begins to require societal complexification, social stratification, and hierarchy, to say nothing of property rights and enforcement mechanisms; as populations grow beyond the carrying capacity of their local bioregions and as weapons develop to secure or protect new territories, the path of destruction has been lain. Necessary, inexorable complexification of society is underway. Collapse is then only a question of *when, not if.*

Perhaps one day humanity will learn this lesson, but I hold little confidence. Thus I shall not waste my time or yours this evening by making an elaborate case. If you want the details you should try to find a copy of my book. It may still exist in one of your makeshift libraries. If you do find the book, you will find it clear and compelling. I hope you give it the attention it deserves and read it with the same intensity with which it was written. If you do, our minds will meet.

I must commence by saying that there is something rather contrived about the horror and disgust with which some of you have interpreted the Great Die-Off and the acts which precipitated it. I say contrived because a Great Die-Off was inevitable, due to the nature of the complex, military-industrial regime that had emerged since the industrial revolution, but which had its seeds planted in the Neolithic revolution some ten thousand years ago. All the suffering caused by the release of Hemlock-42 was already part of the human destiny—perhaps suffering of even *greater* magnitude, since the swiftness of the virus was arguably more compassionate than a slow civilisational collapse, which would have produced an alternative die-off caused by famine, war, and disease.

Why pretend to be horrified when things would have been worse had there been no intervention? If a man is falling from a tall building, would it be so wrong to shoot him out of mercy as he fell? Please shoot me if ever I find myself in such an unprosperous descent, and I promise to offer you the same courtesy. Professor Senjen merely shot the falling man of civilisation. Let us not be so simple minded as to call it murder. That would be a category mistake. Only the naïve child objects as the parent puts down the fatally injured household pet. The enlightened parent proceeds, and ought to proceed, despite the objections, out of mercy and love. So let us not act under the false consciousness of herd morality; let us not condemn Senjen and his colleagues, who sooner deserve our commendation. The times called for a temporary suspension of ordinary ethics—like when Abraham lifted the knife to kill his son—and the subtler minds among you will see this complex truth.

Many of you seem to conceive of human history as being some ten thousand years old, forgetting that great apes came down from the trees and began walking on two feet several million years ago. Even creatures more anatomically similar to ourselves were around hundreds of thousands of years ago. What arrogance it is to assume that these 'pre-historical' creatures, as you describe them, did not live rich, human lives, simply because they did not have gadgets and government. Can not the simplest child derive the deepest pleasure from the simplest things—splashing in water or playing with an animal? Could not our species find spiritual riches in an unencumbered walk in the woods or the embrace of a neighbour? Does any human work of art compare to the sublime vista of a sunset or sunrise? All this and much more was available to the pre-historic beast, who lived in what has been called the 'original affluent society'. What more do we need for this miracle of existence to be seen for what it is: a gift embedded in a warning! Do not overreach or it will end in tragedy. Live in humble simplicity and humanity can thrive into the deep future.

Mr Isaac Smith spoke just now with much enthusiasm and apparent sophistication about the promise and potential of advanced technology and human ingenuity. His claim was that technologies and the pricing mechanisms of markets could resolve the many social and ecological contradictions of industrial civilisation, and thus, so his logic went, the intervention of Hemlock-42 was unnecessary. He spoke with particular fervour about nuclear power, amongst the most complex technologies known in the Before Time. But his defence was so ridden with flaws and distortions that it took some considerable powers of self-control to restrain myself from interjecting midway through each sentence—or simply abandoning this discourse. We let him speak, presumably for his benefit, for it certainly wasn't for ours.

My intention is not to be rude. Let us take a moment to step through his defence. We were reminded that fossil fuels are finite and their combustion was a primary contribution to climatic instability. So far so good. He was fairly critical of the ability of renewable energy technologies to replace the fossil energy foundations of civilisation, and thus jumped to the conclusion that saving that civilisation required nuclear power. It is indeed a power-dense and relatively low-carbon energy source. What is not to like? I shall tell you.

First of all, despite his claims about the speed at which nuclear energy could scale, he lacked perspective. Saying that some nations historically had partially decarbonised their electricity grid in a decade or two was one thing—again, true so far as it went. But thinking that nuclear could therefore scale to replace most or all of the total energy demands of a growing, complex civilisation is another. There were merely four or five hundred nuclear power plants on Earth when I was a boy. Replacing global energy demand would have required around 15,000 such power plants. If future energy demand was to be met with nuclear, by now we'd have needed more than 25,000.

Where were these nuclear plants going to go? On the edge of your settlement? I don't think so. The public was terrified of nuclear power. Whether that fear was legitimate or illegitimate is beside the point. Scaling nuclear in the world *as it was* simply was never going to happen, and so promoting nuclear became nothing but a dangerous distraction. Far from being the practice of *realpolitik*, as Isaac Smith contended, nuclear advocacy was a dead-end strategy that sought to save a civilisation that could not be saved. It would take ten years or more to get a single nuclear power plant through planning to completion, almost all of them being produced grossly over budget. How then could nuclear hope to make a material differ-ence to climate change mitigation? It couldn't. There was not time.

The proper response was radical reduction in energy demand and the embrace of radically simpler ways to live. I admit this was just as unlikely as a global deployment of nuclear power, but it had the advantage of being far more coherent. In any case, embracing radical simplicity as a means of preparing for the collapse of techno-indus-trial society made sense no matter what, since collapse was on its way. It was too late to aim for sustainability; by that stage astute social strategists would have focused exclusively on building resil-ience. Might as well embrace our fate, no? As one old philosopher wrote: 'When a dog runs at you, whistle for him.'

But—what's the phrase?—we were damned if we didn't and we were damned if we did. That is to say, more worrying than the *inability* of nuclear to scale was the risk that nuclear *did indeed begin to scale,* only to have civilisation collapse or degenerate into a new world war—the former being an inevitability and the latter being a very real likelihood as resource scarcity intensified. Suppose, for instance, there were thousands of new nuclear power plants in operation by 2050, helping to mitigate the worst climate impacts. If a global population in pursuit of limitless affluence was continuing to brutally degrade every forest, plain, mountain, and waterway, then ecosystemic collapse would sooner or later, probably sooner, bring an end to civilisation, even if climate change didn't play a significant role.

In such a scenario, what then of the legacy of nuclear power? What happens to those many thousands of nuclear power plants when they become the focus of military targets or when civilisational collapse means they are no longer being maintained and cared for? I will tell you what would happen: nuclear Armageddon. Meltdowns, radiation, toxicity, and possibly a nuclear winter that ended most if not all life on Earth. In a global civilisation as fragile and contradictory as the world we knew in the Before Time, it would have been insane to build thousands of nuclear power stations. Even today I am tempted to despair thinking of what has become of the nuclear power plants that our species did build—and what horrors their deterioration may yet wreak upon us, abandoned in the After World. Anyone who had any insight into the likelihood of collapse or global war simply would never have considered a far greater nuclear rollout a sensible option. The risks far outweighed any 'clean energy' potential it could have, for a time, provided. The further problem was that nuclear energy was siphoning billions and billions of dollars away from the more fundamental task of managing the inevitable descent of techno-industrial civilisation.

The same flawed 'balancing of risks' applies to Mr Smith's deluded faith in geoengineering. Suppose spraying the stratosphere with sulphate aerosols managed to reflect enough sunlight to manage climate change for a few years or even a few decades. That may be fine, so long as civilisation is sufficiently stable to maintain the dispersion of such aerosols. But any clear and honest thinker who could see the contradictions inherent in industrial civilisation and who could see that its collapse was inevitable, would have dismissed geoengineering the climate in this fashion as dangerously reckless. Within a few years of civilisation collapsing the failure to maintain sulphate aerosol dispersion would have catapulted climate warming to where it would have been had geoengineering never occurred, leading to a relatively sudden spike in temperatures which would have devastated agricultural systems and led to a great die-off of an even more horrific form. Sometimes the so-called cure is worse than the poison.

To be frank, I shudder at the thought of nuclear innovation (or any technology) giving humanity unlimited free, clean energy—energy 'too cheap to meter'. We had not, and have not, the maturity to wield such awesome power. We would have simply murdered Gaia faster and more efficiently. Gross inequalities of wealth would have remained under a clean energy capitalism and so too, no doubt, would the consumer cultures that celebrated nice things as the ultimate good. Cheap, clean energy without an ethical revolution would have been worse than what clean energy sought to avoid.

All that said, I have not yet unpacked the fundamental error of Mr Smith's defence of nuclear power and geoengineering, which relates to his underlying assumptions. It is clear that Mr Smith was trying to figure out how to save complex, globalised consumer capitalism from self-destructing. But what he totally failed to see is that he had posed the wrong question, so his answer was always going to be wrong, irrelevant, or otherwise fundamentally misconceived.

The question of the Before Time should not have been: how can we make consumer capitalism just and sustainable? That was like trying to cure a terminal patient or fix an irremediable machine. It was a waste of time. The questions of the Before Time ought to have been (and for us, ought to be): what does a just and sustainable civilisation look like? And how can we give rise to it? And this naturally returns me to the notion of anarcho-primitivism, which, as I have already proposed, is the only form of life consistent with a 'deep future' civilisation. Sustainability, after all, does not mean viable for several decades or even centuries. Sustainability means developing a way of life that is viable for thousands, no, for millions, of years.

Of course, the material simplicity of a non-affluent, low-tech existence need not delimit our existential ambitions, provided we look inward *to being* for our cravings for infinity and divinity, not outward *to having*. Radical simplicity is perfectly consistent with happiness, peace, nature mysticism, community, and love. As we all now know, we don't need computers, planes, and industrial agriculture to live well. Yes, the anarcho-primitivist derives his or her technology from the resources found within the bioregion. As we have proven, we can make our own mud huts, clay pots, fire pits, needles, and other basic tools. But not far beyond this threshold we must choose voluntary simplicity, not involuntary complexification, and ensure that our populations do not grow beyond the carrying capacity of our local bioregions. We should reject any development of a large centralised state and instead organise and self-govern through participatory democratic practices in small communities. Only by adopting these basic societal forms and practices can we hope to live in accordance with Natural Law.

Before closing let me say a word on human nature, which no doubt some of you will maintain is inconsistent with a 'simpler way' civilisation. That is, some people will insist that humans are greedy, self-interested, competitive, war-like, power-hungry, and inherently desiring of material and technological advancement, and so, the objection might go, anarcho-primitivism is unsuitable for our species. Leaving aside the historical fact that anarcho-primitivism actually is the dominant form of life throughout history, there are two equally compelling philosophical points to make on this issue.

The first is to question whether the very notion of human nature is even coherent. I have my doubts. After all, no matter what urges and desires may come to us by virtue of our evolutionary constitution, the fact remains that at every point we are free to manage those urges and desires as we see fit. It follows, as the existentialists in the Before Time argued, that we will be what we make of ourselves and nothing else, or at least, that we can always make something new out of what we have been made into. Put simply, there is no such thing as human nature. We must invent our nature through our actions and decisions, and to deny that radical freedom is to act in bad faith; it is to say that our actions are determined by our biological nature when in fact they are self-determined by our will. And thus, if human nature does not exist, there can be no human nature objection to anarcho-primitivism.

But even if this philosophical point is too subtle for some of you, there is an alternative way to respond to the human nature objection. And that is to accept it, but to show that it does not lead to objectionable conclusions. This too can be shown to be the case. If consumer culture had proven to be a way of life in which people were genuinely flourishing, one might well conclude that self-interested human beings would lead people to pursue material affluence, even if this deprived others of basic material provisions and even if it ultimately was degrading the natural environment. But all the evidence suggested that most people in consumer cultures were overworked in meaningless jobs, disconnected from nature, dominated by technology, alienated from their communities, and poor in mental and physical health. On that basis, people driven by self-interest would have recognised, if they were thinking clearly, that consumerism was a disastrous social experiment that was not producing the happiness and sense of purpose promised to them in the glossy advertisements. That would demand an alternative—not because people were altruistic, but because they cared for their own wellbeing.

But more fundamentally, if people were sufficiently self-interested to care about their wellbeing and the wellbeing of their offspring, then clearly it was in our own self-interest not to destroy the ecosystems which we depended on to live. And so we see, both in the near term and in the long term, an enlightened self-interest would have rejected the cultures and systems of techno-industrial society and demanded a radical alternative. In terms of my substantive contribution this evening, that can be my closing point: anarcho-primitivism—the only way of life compatible with a 'deep future' civilisation—is in our enlightened self-interest. I call on you all to build this Natural Law into your emerging societies in the After World. If you do not, the process of complexification will lead to the same result every other complex society arrived at: collapse. Let us have the wisdom to choose otherwise.

As for what should be done with Durruk Senjen. What is done is done. Let us ignore him to death. We still have problems enough of our own.

On saying these closing words, Jack Zanzer walks slowly and carefully through the mass of people seated amongst the dancing shadows, and leaves the stadium via the Southern exit, disappearing into the night. The cold and emotionless delivery of his address somehow suppresses the visceral reactions evoked by earlier speakers, even though it is clear by the look on many people's twisted faces that they are bottling up thoughts and emotions they have not yet been able to digest or express. Others are seen nodding and sharing words of agreement for what they have just heard.

9. Dying with Dignity

Dr Jacob Jade was a member of the board of the Association of Concerned Earth Scientists, however no one ever asked him to participate in the Hemlock-42 agenda. Senjen and others knew perfectly well that Jade would never have offered his support.

Jacob Jade was a deeply empathetic man—he felt the suffering of people and animals as if it were his own—yet it was not clear to him or to others whether this was a blessing or a curse. In part this character trait was the driver of his noble work in conservation biology and habitat restoration, work for which he had become justly famous in his lifetime. On the other hand, the intensity of his empathy would sometimes distract his attention from arguably more pressing matters, like the time he failed to submit a promising grant application for $6 million because he was nursing a sick dog he found lying in the gutter near his house. As things transpired, he wasn't able to save the dog, and one is left to imagine what good he could have done with that funding. In retrospect he recognised that his emotional state narrowed his vision of the world and interfered with his logical or rational faculties. But he was who he was and there was no changing that. 'Abstract thought can make a person blind and cruel,' he wrote in one of his journals.

Jade spent his final days nursing his sick wife, Francesca—offering her palliative care as malignant cancers took hold of her body. Because her diagnosis was terminal, she had decided that she would euthanise herself by refusing to eat, rather than extend her life unnecessarily with all the pain and suffering that would bring to herself and others. She asked her husband to feed her only liquids so that she could consciously and deliberately leave life at her own time, on her own terms. She faded away in relative peace less than a week before Hemlock-42 was released.

Two weeks later, the virus had taken Jacob from this world also, perhaps mercifully, since by that stage he was suffering a nervous breakdown that had pushed him to the edge of insanity. Death brought him welcome relief.

Monica Jade is the daughter of Jacob and Francesca, their only child. She was eleven when she watched first her mother, then her father, leave this world. Like many other children, she survived the Great Die-Off only to find herself alone in the world, without parents or family, forced to make her way by whatever means possible. It was an intensely insecure and difficult time, taking her from the brink of starvation, through moments of good fortune, joy, and grace, to a period of three years where she was essentially working as a slave on a farm merely to survive.

The material and spiritual conditions of her existence are now much better, living in a small and vibrant community of poet-farmers. But for everyone alive today who lived through the Great Die-Off, including Monica, the memories remain, like scar tissue of the soul. Those memories cannot be ignored or forgotten. Repressing them only produces unpredictable neuroses. At best, they can be slowly and mindfully digested in the hope of finding the dark gold; finding the shadows that prove there must be light, somewhere.

Tonight, Monica finds herself standing before the vast crowd gathered in the stadium. The fire, which earlier in the night had reached upward toward the heavens, has reduced to a quiet burn, mostly embers. She had prepared a speech but presently her mind had gone completely blank, so she stands there silently, trying to recall her opening line. A poet lost for words, she musters the courage to simply begin speaking in her thick accent of unknown origin, trusting that she will find her voice soon enough.

Good evening everyone. My name is Monica Jade. I live in Starfallen Grove, a small farming community near the foot of the Eastern Mount. I'm very nervous tonight, you can probably tell, so forgive me if I stumble or stutter. I'm not used to speaking publicly like this, but I hope I am able to share my thoughts and feelings coherently enough, I mean, even though those thoughts and feelings are rushing through me as I speak, uncontrollably, I have to admit, like a river threatening to burst its banks after a storm. Already my eyes are wet in anticipation of what I might have to say, and the lump in my throat seems to be growing. But I'll try my best, you know, do my best, to make sense. Thank you for your charity and patience. I feel some important things have been overlooked tonight.

Please don't assume you know what I think or feel just because some of you may have known my parents. Although my father has deeply shaped who I am—both through nature and nurture—I am not my father and I am not my mother. I am my own person. It may surprise you to hear that as I listened to our speakers this evening, I found the defendants so often more compelling than the prosecutors. Supported by my own extensive readings, and through exposure to oral history, it is now clear to me that the crises of industrial civilisation—especially the ecological crises—were far deeper and more brutal than most people before the Great Die-Off recognised or were willing to admit.

I suspect that even my father, a prominent conservation biologist, under-estimated the nature of the forces that were encroaching ever more violently into the wild spaces which animated his spirit. You can imagine that dinnertime conversation in my household would often turn to my father's work fighting a particular development project, or responding to a particular weather event, a flood or a fire, perhaps, that had devastated a natural reserve and threatened this species or that species in new ways. I could always hear the passion and compassion in his voice; his resentment in seeing a wetland drained and covered in concrete; his anger at another old-growth forest being cleared for urban sprawl; as well as the vibrancy and joy in his voice as he described seeing a rare moth or a frog that he considered more magnificent than Notre Dame or any work of Shakespeare or Mozart. He loved the wild as much as he despised the shopping mall that destroyed it.

But it wasn't until I was an adult that I came to see that my father seemed to think, or acted as if, these encroachments on nature were unrelated instances that could be coherently resisted on their own, individual terms. Do not get me wrong. I loved, respected, and admired him. He lived his truth and his duty as he understood it, and his memory still inspires me; it gets me out of bed in the morning. He was animated with a moral conviction that seems to have been so sorely lacking in the Age of Empire. But in the end, the way he fought back, the way he tried to contribute to the betterment of our society, was like the doctor who only treated symptoms and never thought of addressing the cause. And so busy was he reacting to symptoms that he wasn't able to see that the symptoms were so many and so powerful that responding to them one by one was never going to be enough. He was fighting a losing war, but he could never see this because occasionally he would win a battle, giving him false hope.

So, as I say, my sympathies tonight lie at first instance with the defendant, Professor Senjen, and the reasonings of Andrea Lorde and Jack Zanzer, whose various depictions of industrial civilisation and its impacts on the biosphere struck me as far more accurate than their detractors. Empire recognised no limits—*could not recognise any limits*—because that was not in the genetic code of such a globalised economic system, which was ridden with growth imperatives. If money could be made by levelling a forest or destroying topsoil, then by force of its own internal logic Empire would do just that, without a second thought. To save a single tree only to lose wealth or power just didn't make sense. In any case, if one corporation chose not to cut that tree down, then be sure that there would be a line of more desperate and callous corporations waiting with chainsaws in hand. So there was little point trying to conserve it via 'green growth'. The so-called green corporations would simply cut the forest down with chainsaws that ran on bio-diesel, and thereby sleep easy. But the forests were still disappearing, and ever-more species were going extinct.

I guess this speaks to my further sympathies with the defendants. Not only did they accurately measure the extent of ecological overshoot, they also forcefully explained why the conventional forms of resistance—whether living simply, buying 'green', lobbying one's member of parliament, or organising a protest—were never going to slow the march of Empire. On these points, Andrea Lorde spoke with devastating power. Sure, spend your money conscientiously—buy organic! donate to charities! invest in solar!—but know that infinitely more money was in the hands of people who just didn't give a fuck about nature or justice. Forgive my cursing, but come on, people. 'Voting with your money' was like entering a battle where one person has a candle and on the other side several people have flamethrowers. One should know very well who is going to win. If you only have a candle and the rest have flamethrowers, don't fight fire with fire—or money with money. It's not just sad, it's stupid.

The same goes for the 'simple living' movement, more broadly. One can hardly criticise this strategy in itself, because all the evidence suggests that these counter-culturalists genuinely lived happier, freer, healthier lives than those desperately trying to win the rat race. All power to them! Stepping out of the rush made eminently good sense—as a way of life. But as a political strategy or environmental strategy, let us not delude ourselves. Capitalism was quite capable of accommodating the resistance of a bunch of frugal hedonists, and in fact the system was delighted to sell those hippies their solar ovens and alternative medicines which they needed to participate in their tribal practices. But any rational observer should have seen that most people were not going to join the simple living movement—not by choice, anyway. People may not have drawn much comfort or any meaning from their 'nice things' or 'high status jobs', but in a culture that celebrated materialism and consumerism, there just wasn't much chance at all of mobilising people, en masse, in opposition. Voluntary simplicity made perfectly good sense in theory—literally, it made *perfectly* good sense—but in practice, at some point the evidence-based political strategist should have concluded that it was a dead-end. As one writer of the time so aptly noted, people would never 'riot for austerity'. After all, the entire march of history was arguably an attempt to escape material austerity and attain more material wealth—although, we now know, this very search for material wealth was also laying the path to extinction.

Of course, this leads naturally to the absurdity of hoping for a 'top down' political response to the problems of industrial civilisaiton. People didn't want less stuff, so no political party would campaign to provide less stuff. I'm afraid it's that simple. People wanted more—both the rich and the poor. More, more, more. Those who said that they didn't want more were delusional or being insincere. And politicians want power, so they would never do anything that would risk offending a materialistic citizenry that they needed to vote them into power. Furthermore, governments were always short of money, there was never enough, so they would always work to grow the tax base—not deliberately shrink it. Indeed, given that human beings have been eternally at war, no government would choose to reduce its military strength by deliberately reducing the size of its economy for environmental reasons. It's not much good saving the environment if that only led to one's enemies being able to invade and occupy your land.

So however coherent it was to call for 'degrowth' of the overgrown economies in the hope of moving toward a 'one planet' civilisation, it was never going to happen. The logic of complex societies would never allow it. Never. Industrial civilisation was destined—essentially as a matter of structural inevitability—to grow itself into a collapse situation. History confirms this grim diagnosis, as Mr Zanzer stated so clearly. A Great Simplification was inevitable, one way or another. And here we are.

The question we are faced with this evening—the question we have been faced with ever since industrial civilisation was brought to its knees—is how should one have acted, what should one have done, in the midst of a society that was, as I say, destined for ecological (and thus humanitarian) Armageddon. More specifically, what was one to do when all the conventional modes of response seemed so utterly hopeless. As I reflect on the acts which led to the Great Die-Off—specifically, the deliberate release of Hemlock-42—I find myself genuinely torn between, on the one hand, the love of Earth and nature which motivated Senjen and, on the other hand, abhorrence and disgust at the monstrous acts which he and his collaborators committed.

How are we to resolve these contradictory tensions—these tensions which I am sure many of you feel in the depths of your nature. Let us not pretend, at least, that there are simple answers here. Industrial civilisation was in the midst of killing Mother Earth, there is no denying that. If things had gone on for much longer, ecosystemic collapse was the 'white swan' lying around the next bend in the river. Billions would have died as a result, perhaps in even more horrendous and barbaric ways than Hemlock-42 brought us. And yet humanity was never given the chance to avert that worst-case scenario, because Senjen and his team intervened in their pre-emptive strike. They were not prepared to wait any longer, to see any more old-growth forests, any more beautiful species, be expunged from this planet so mindlessly and recklessly. And given the extreme unlikelihood (essentially zero chance) of any smooth, rational transition away from industrial civilisation, one can certainly see why Senjen and his team intervened as they did. After all, if protecting the Earth from further destruction was the *ultimate goal*, then I am prepared to concede that their strategy was probably the most coherent means of bringing humanity back into balance with natural ecosystems.

I can sense that some of you are shocked by that admission, but please let me finish, because I will now explain why I nevertheless condemn Senjen and his team for their actions, *despite* the nobility of their goals and *despite* the effectiveness of their methods. It is all very well for them to have a noble goal and effective means, but like other critics, I am firmly of the view that the death, suffering, and violence they caused enacting their plan was so horrendous that no 'end' could justify such means.

That said, I do not stand before you merely to repeat the lines of reasoning already presented. I do not base my condemnation on the fact that this was a violation of human rights—although human rights were clearly violated. It seems to me that Senjen and his collaborators were seeking to protect a more inclusive body of rights, and could cogently argue, as Senjen in fact argued, that if rights are what we care for then the release of Hemlock-42 was justified. I feel no need to draw my own conclusions here, on which paradigm of understanding—human rights or rights of nature—is more appropriate in assessing the matter of Senjen's culpability. Ultimately, I feel that question is beside the point, in ways I shall explain.

Furthermore, I do not base my conviction of Senjen on the grounds that there were alternative, less violent means to achieve the same end of ecological harmony. Although I wish there had been alternative means, I substantially agree with Andrea Lorde that to stop the violence of industrial civilisation, only violent resistance would do. As I have said, green lifestyles, technological innovation, and progressive politics were never going to turn the ship of industrial civilisation around before it crashed into the rocks of its own making.

So here is where I depart from previous critics and defendants. While I accept all other methods were destined to be ineffective, I nevertheless conclude the very nature of the murderous acts which restored ecological balance to Earth were so vile and repugnant that they could never be justified—no matter how bad things got and no matter how effectively they achieved their social and ecological goals. To argue that murdering more than seven billion people was an act of justice and environmentalism simply defies every thread in my moral fabric, and I believe that every one of you would agree with me if you were able to wash your minds clean of the rhetorical arguments of all speakers that have gone before me. They have merely muddied the waters by invoking false logic, noble sounding goals, and alternative strategies. Most of them missed the more fundamental consideration: no 'end', however noble, could justify the method of mass murder. None. Absolutely none—and you all know it in your hearts. Even as we look around and see this derelict city being gracefully retaken by nature, this does not for one minute suggest that the mass murder which permitted this rewilding was justified. It was not. No utilitarian calculus—no serving of a 'greater good'—can justify the Great Die-Off.

Some of you will have noticed the darkness in my vision, but to ensure I am understood I must now bring it to the surface. Although I condemn those who released Hemlock-42, you have also heard that I have rejected arguments which maintained that alternative strategies could have achieved the goal of ecological reconciliation. In other words, I reject the strategy of bringing down industrial civilisaiton even as I accept that ecological destruction could not be stopped via other means. It follows that I believe the tragedy of the human predicament was to live through the continued destruction of nature and the eventual collapse of industrial civilisation with the greatest dignity and kindness we could muster. Yes, industrial civilisation was dying, inevitably dying, and killing Gaia as it did so, inevitably killing Gaia, but that just laid down our most fundamental task: to die with dignity; to collapse consciously. Senjen and his collaborators violated that injunction in the grossest possible way. They have eternally contaminated the human spirit, the human story. And for that they can never be forgiven. Their acts will never be forgotten.

This all resonates very personally with me too. Before the Great Die-Off, my mother, like industrial civilisation, was terminally sick. My father could have murdered her in her sleep and thus reduced her suffering. Instead, he took care of her as the cancers took hold. He did not try to save her, since she could not be saved. So, he did everything he could to help her die with dignity—and thereby, himself, live a dignified life. He continued to live in the spirit of love and kindness, and in full knowledge that his actions could not change her fate, her destiny. Hopelessly, he held her hand as she died, and I find this very personal story an apt analogy for our current question. What I am arguing is that mass murder was not a dignified act, could never be a dignified act, no matter the context, no matter the prospects of reward, even ecological salvation. Things were essentially hopeless, but that did not justify the release of Hemlock-42. Hopelessness just called for infinite resignation, to be followed by a revolution of love, an approach to life which would find meaning in the small moments of spiritual connection and joy on the path of civilisational descent.

And perhaps this is the type of reasoning which motivated my father in his conservation work. I had always assumed he was trying to 'win' by engaging in his small battles against the plague of corporate development. But perhaps he knew very well he wasn't going to win the war. Perhaps he wasn't *trying* to win. Perhaps he was just doing what his conscience demanded of him. If something is destroying what you love, resist that destruction with commitment and dignity—but recognise that there are lines one should not cross when trying to save what you love, because if you gain the world but lose your soul, then everything is lost. Maintain the integrity of one's soul, I say, even if that means embracing collapse with defiant kindness. This is the psychology of hopelessness which I feel should have shaped human consciousness. We should have gone down with the ship, like the string quartet which supposedly played as the *Titanic* sank, back in the Before Time. You may have heard the story.

Arguably there is a deeper lesson in the approach of that string quartet, concerning the role of art in a dying civilisation. Neither art nor science nor politics could have provoked the transformations needed to avoid the apocalypse of industrial civilisation, but to my mind that just means the role of the artist is magnified, as creative imaginations are tasked with interpreting and understanding civilisational descent in terms that give meaning to the inevitability of suffering; give sense to the pain we feel on the far side of Empire's collapse. At this turn in the story, the therapeutic or even spiritual role of art must take precedence over its political function. The very term 'apocalypse' has a dual meaning, not simply referring to the 'end of the world' but also signifying 'a great unveiling or disclosure' of knowledge. It will be the artist, not the scientist, I contend, who will contribute most to the human understanding of this disclosure. Rather than wallow helplessly as humanity descends into barbarism, let us hope that our musicians, artists, novelists, story-tellers, and poets are up to the task of weaving narratives of human and ecological suffering into a meaningful web of solidarity and compassion—and thereby, perhaps, give birth to a new golden age of Grecian tragedy that offers both an education and cleansing of the emotions and passions in these turbulent and uncertain times. Perhaps that is the new dawn that lies beyond this dark hour.

Let me end on a rather different note. We know our self-righteous defendant claims to have acted as he did to 'save nature' or to 'save the planet'. Well, I put it to you that nature and the planet were always going to survive. Earth did not need saving; Gaia would have survived no matter how brutally we treated her. Of course it was tragic what we were doing to the diversity of species—destroying their habitats and casually sending them to extinction. But life on Earth has a deep future—the sun will shine for billions of years. So even if humanity had changed the face of Gaia so drastically that our own form of life would have gone extinct, life itself would not have gone extinct, but would have evolved. New creatures would have emerged. Over tens of thousands of years the climate would have readjusted—perhaps a million years after we had gone extinct there would be no evidence that we were ever here. Nature will survive us. We need Gaia, but she doesn't need us.

My point is that Senjen and his collaborators were out to save nature when what we really needed to be doing was saving ourselves—not in the sense of saving our destructive civilisation. That was beyond redemption; it was always coming down. Rather, we needed to maintain whatever was left of our moral legitimacy. As I have argued, in a civilisation destined to collapse from its own internal contradictions, why murder billions merely to hasten a descent that was already on the cards? Why participate in such ungodly acts merely to bring forward a great rebalancing that was coming no matter what? As a species, we now have to live with Senjen's legacy and that is a stain that can never be removed.

I guess the only other thing I should address is the question of sentencing. No doubt there will be a range of judgements concerning the legitimacy of the acts under consideration. For those who agree that the surviving perpetrator is guilty, the question arises as to how he should be held accountable. Tonight, we have heard sentencing recommendations of death, exile, and eye-gouging. These recommendations strike me as inadequate or misconceived. Guilty though they are, I feel impelled to advocate for pardoning Senjen and those who aided and abetted him. No doubt he has already suffered enough to pay for the crimes he committed. Life, we all know, is suffering. Why participate in this curse unnecessarily?

I therefore welcome Senjen to come and live with me and my community at Starfallen Grove. This is not an act of forgiveness but an act of unconditional mercy and kindness. I can confirm that I have been given the authority from my community to offer this invitation, and I hope that all of you present tonight can find it in your hearts to show mercy at this critical juncture in our moral journey. We will never forget, of course—we should never forget—and there is little point in considering forgiveness, since those whom we might forgive do not acknowledge their guilt and therefore do not want our forgiveness.

This fire is dying. Perhaps you are as tired as I am. It is time to move on—to look forward, not backwards.

Monica Jade, showing clear signs of emotional exhaustion, returns to her seat on the outer edges of the gathering. The unfiltered compassion of her speech seems to have quietened people's emotions and the crowd remains quiet as Monica finds her place. En route she passes Zola Eblo, who has gathered another armful of branches with which to refuel the fire. She casts them directly into the pit and with a flick of her cloak she pushes enough oxygen into the embers to reignite the fire. She then takes another armful of wood and throws it atop the dancing flames, before turning to address the people once more.

10. Violence and Self-Image

Let us pray:

> *Blue Star, We are Thy Tears, The Guidance of Gaia, We Seek;*
> *Great Spirit, the Fire in our Eyes, Before Thee, We Speak.*

Beneath this divine night sky, I thank you, one and all, for your attention and patience. Unless there are any objections, our ceremony will draw to a close. Tonight we have been exposed to a diverse and complex array of interpretations, and it is a challenge to keep all the emotionally charged issues fresh in one's mind. Perhaps it would be useful for me to spend a short time attempting to restate, in the simplest possible terms, the variety of perspectives shared this evening. We will then face the question of how to respond, both as individuals and as a community of communities. I will attempt to do each case due justice, albeit in summary form.

Our friend Immanuel Wright opened substantive proceedings this evening by presenting a brief but clear statement, arguing that the release of Hemlock-42 was a deliberate and calculated act, intended to kill billions of human beings, and thus one which violated human rights to life, liberty, and the pursuit of happiness. He argued that universal standards of moral decency and intuition should compel us to see these acts as acts of murder—nay, as acts of terrorism, plain and simple—for which he argued the only appropriate sentence would be the death penalty. This opening prosecution had powerful common-sense appeal, you might agree—but had it oversimplified the situation somewhat? Or had Mr Wright in fact captured the situation with the simplicity it deserved?

In response, Professor Durruk Senjen defended the central role he played in the events precipitating the Great Die-Off. Far from acknowledging guilt, Senjen turned the opening critique on its head, defending the release of Hemlock-42 as a means of *protecting* rights, not in *violation* of them. To make this case he expanded the notion of 'rights' to include not only the class of living humans and all future generations, but also the broader community of species which he argued also had a right to inhabit our majestic planet without threat of extinction. This shifted the terms of analysis and arguably opened up space for alternative evaluations of what had occurred.

Professor Senjen, to his credit, did not deny the tragedy of the Great Die-Off. He simply insisted that releasing the virus was a necessary intervention to protect the rights of nature, including the rights of future generations—including ourselves, presumably—to live in balance and harmony with Gaia. And here we are today, the beneficiaries of Hemlock-42. But were there not alternative, less violent ways to achieve the same end? Should Senjen be seen as a self-righteous terrorist? Or conversely, was he simply brave enough to act 'beyond good and evil' on hard questions which many of us would sooner have avoided out of fear or complacency? Senjen declared that ordinary people acting in ordinary ways were being complicit in a system that was doing great violence, and thus they had no right to conceive of themselves as non-violent. Paradoxically, he claimed his deathly acts were necessary to minimise violence.

At this point Mohandria Bentharma stood before us, adding much depth and sophistication to a contested analysis that I could see was already pulling people in various directions. She argued that there were indeed alternative, non-violent ways to achieve harmony and balance on Earth. Imperfect though democracy was in the Before Time, Aunty Bentharma nevertheless insisted that democratic politics, peaceful civil disobedience, and participation in progressive social movements provided all the necessary tools for the non-violent transformation of society. People have the power to change the world, she argued, so social enlightenment and political struggle could have resolved the ecological crises of industrial civilisation without resort to violence and murder.

Indeed, Aunty Bentharma argued that the forces of revolt were already rising in the Before Time. Enlightened transformation was never going to be easy and success was not certain, but she maintained that the mere possibility of success meant that the release of Hemlock-42 was an undemocratic, elitist, and violent intervention that defied all respect for deliberative, collective decision making. She supported her democratic reasoning with a simple but forceful utilitarian calculus: billions had suffered painful deaths through exposure to Hemlock-42 and suffered through experiencing the deaths of loved ones; the 'good' that was achieved through this drastic intervention was an insufficient counterbalance to the vast suffering it wrought upon the world. Had the guilt of Senjen and his colleagues now been firmly established? Or had Aunty Bentharma been idealistic in her hopes for a transformative democratic politics?

It was time for the Youth Council to have its say, and Andrea Lorde was invited to offer her thoughts as a representative. Although always respectful of Aunty Bentharma, Andrea subjected the defence of democratic politics to a scathing and forceful critique. She accepted that transformative change was a *theoretical possibility* within democratic societies in the Before Time, but she insisted that we have not gathered here to assess questions of theory but questions of practice. Was a radical 'simple living' movement likely—in the real world—to have revolutionised cultures of consumption and organised collectively for progressive structural change? One might have hoped for that with naïve optimism, but Andrea made a case that this was all politically idealistic and blind to what was actually happening. In the absence of some other intervention, the most likely outcome of democratic politics playing out was ecological (and thus humanitarian) catastrophe. There were indeed people participating in marginalised countercultures, but every day Gaia was being degraded further by an industrial civilisation that recognised no limits. At some point, those who sought ecological balance needed to ask hard questions about what strategy was most likely to be effective.

When one loses all hope in democratic politics, what remains aside from violent resistance? In the end Andrea argued that a civilisation as inherently violent as Empire could only be stopped with violence. But she insisted this was no casual celebration of green rage. The position was defended in relation to an ethics of self-defence. If what you love and depend on is being brutally destroyed—whether that is your mother or Mother Earth herself—you have a right, and perhaps an obligation, to fight back in protection, surely? If future generations or non-human species cannot fight back, then that responsibility falls on those who have the capacity to act. That was the essential line of argument Andrea Lorde presented in defence of Professor Senjen and his colleagues, and she may well be right that her very existence is owed to their deathly but strategic intervention. The logic, I admit, is powerful, yet I was still left uncertain of the veracity of the conclusion. An argument can be valid but not sound. Could this be such a case?

The moral situation became even more complicated when Andrea deconstructed the utilitarian critique from Mohandria Bentharma and turned it into a utilitarian defence: sure, Andrea said, the Great Die-Off caused unfathomable suffering, but ultimately it provided the conditions for human beings, other species, and ecosystems to flourish into the deep future. In short, she insisted that there would have been even more suffering had Hemlock-42 *not* been released. Was the intervention thus justified on utilitarian grounds? Perhaps it is too early to tell.

Our next speaker was Isaac Smith, who insisted that it is not too early to tell. He argued unreservedly that the release of Hemlock-42 was wrong, on the grounds that market society and technological inno-vation had the potential to resolve the deepest of ecological pres-sures and social justice concerns without such violence. Humans had essentially become gods, he said, by inducing the Anthropocene, but if we had the power to damage the most important Earth systems, we had the power to fix them. A case could be made that, in the Before Time, humans already had the technological capacity to solve the crises of civilisation. For example, Mr Smith held up nuclear power as a mature technology that could provide clean and affordable energy to power civilisation and thereby resolve climate change. There was no need, he insisted, for revolution, and collapse was clearly avoidable. If necessary, we even had the knowledge and capacity to geoengineer the climate to ensure it didn't overheat. In short, Mr Smith invited us to put faith in the ingenuity of our own species to resolve whatever challenges we faced through technological innovation and application. It was an inspiring self-image, but had he overstated the capacity of technology to save the day? Couldn't we just as likely hold up technology as the cause of our global and existential predicaments? Again, I could sense that many were left as confused and uncertain as I was.

Mr Smith, not relenting, made a further point in support of reform. He accepted that the reality of capitalism in the Before Time was deeply flawed, but economic theory of the age showed that there were elegant solutions to humanity's most severe problems, and thus the task was not to destroy the system but to refine and regulate it. If certain consumption and production practices were environmentally malignant, then simple pricing mechanisms could shift behaviour in more sustainable directions. Internalise all externalities, he argued. After all, if something is expensive, humans do less of it; they are incentivised to find or develop substitutes. Given the inherent selfishness of human beings, Mr Smith insisted that managing behaviour in this way was not just necessary but the best way to maximise overall wellbeing, including resolving environmental degradation. And so we see the utilitarian critique returning here, in a different form, this time in a defence of free markets and technology. Again, the logic seemed sound within its own terms of reference. But that begged the very question.

At this stage Jack Zanzer entered the discussion, presenting a radical critique of civilisation and arguing that the only viable mode of existence on the planet is what he calls 'anarcho-primitivism'. His case may be quite fresh in your minds, so I can be particularly brief here. He began by taking the gloss off nuclear energy and geoengineering, listing a range of reasons why such 'cures' threatened to be worse than the poison. If collapse was the most likely future for industrial civilisation, wasn't it grossly irresponsible to deploy nuclear power en masse or conduct risky geoengineering experiments in climate management? In any case, this critical line of inquiry was merely the cutting edge of a broader scepticism toward techno-industrial society. Zanzer stated that complex societies had an inbuilt structural requirement to grow beyond sustainable limits, and he was right to note that the rise and demise of all previous civilisations supported his theory.

If he was right in this diagnosis, then two things seemed to follow. First, the highly complex, industrial civilisation was destined to collapse, and so bringing it down as soon as possible was akin to 'shooting the falling man of civilisation' as an act of mercy. This cast the release of Hemlock-42 in a new light. The second implication was that only a radically simple, low-tech, and primarily non-agriculture civilisation could be sustainable into the deep future. One might find this conclusion difficult to accept, but it is also difficult to find fault in the logic. For millions of years humans lived as hunter-gatherers without degrading ecosystems in unsustainable ways. Yet, in merely a few thousand years of agricultural society, and merely a few hundred years of industrial society, we took ourselves to the edge of ecological apocalypse. To what extent can this evolution toward collapse be considered progress?

Our final contribution this evening came from Monica Jade. Just when I had thought all of the possible perspectives had been presented, this deep thinker opened my mind to a new ethical sensibility. She began by acknowledging what seemed to be a paradoxical position. She accepted that democratic politics, markets, and technology were never going to be able to resolve the contradictions of industrial civilisation. She also accepted that some form of violent resistance—such as the release of Hemlock-42—was the most coherent strategy for restoring balance on Earth. And yet, despite acknowledging that ecological regeneration was a noble goal and despite his having an effective strategy to achieve that goal, Ms Jade nevertheless condemned the actions of Senjen and his collaborators. She argued that no 'end' could justify such horrendous 'means'. Rather than stain our human story with such a violent act, Ms Jade argued that it would have been better to 'die with dignity', as she put it. In other words, she argued that the proper course of action in the midst of an ecocidal civilisation is to be kind, to step as lightly as one can, and try to wash one's hands of industrial violence at every opportunity. She called on us to walk a spiritual path of civilisational collapse; to collapse consciously, one might say. Avoiding collapse was not a sufficient reward for having to live with the stain of billions murdered.

Having to live with the stain of billions murdered...

Zola Eblo paused, having finished her summary. She turned to stare into the fire, as if in trance. So long did she stare that people began to wonder whether the ceremony was officially over. But just as people began to get restless, Zola turned again to the gathered tribes to deliver her final words.

My brothers and sisters of Gaia, if there is one question before us it is this: if you—in your individuality—lived at the peak of industrial civilisation, as some of you did, knowing what it was doing to our planet, and knowing the slim chances of a smooth, evidence-based, progressive response to our crises, what would you have done, if you had a vial of Hemlock-42 in your hands? The system was killing life. The system was violent. Did that justify a violent and deathly response, all things considered?

Zola again turned to stare into the fire. After an indeterminate time, she gathered another handful of branches and threw them onto the growing flames.

My friends, I have a confession to make. I have been honoured to be facilitating the discussion tonight—deeply honoured—but I have been doing so under false pretences. For almost five decades I have been drifting through the After World in search of truth and peace. My life has changed and it seems my appearance has changed sufficiently for those who once knew me to find me unrecognisable. Even my old colleague Professor Senjen seems not to recognise me.

Zola Eblo turns to look at Durruk Senjen and lifts back her hair so that her face is unobstructed. A look of recognition passes over Senjen's face, and several people gasp, but Zola continues before anyone can speak.

Yes, I am your old colleague, Dr Chloe McPherson. I was in the inner circle of the Association of Concerned Earth Scientists that developed and ultimately released Hemlock-42. Indeed, although Durruk, my lost friend, was the primary orchestrator of events, the development of Hemlock-42 was primarily in my hands, being the lead biochemist amongst our activist cell. In fact, it was also lain upon me the burden of walking into the subways of New York to release the first instalment of the virus. I then travelled to the various continents of the world to distribute the virus in strategic places, usually airports, chosen to lead to the widest possible contamination in the shortest possible time. I did so confidently and without remorse or regret, knowing—or thinking I knew—that my inner turmoil was a small price to pay for the glorious reward of ecological balance. For decades I have been troubled by what I did, but for decades I never once felt regret or remorse. Never, that is, until tonight, when I was exposed to perspectives that I had never fully considered—or never let myself consider.

Now, having been exposed to the variety of perspectives both in defence and prosecution of our actions, the confidence I once held in the legitimacy of my role has been shaken to the core. While I am not convinced of the wrongness of my role, my brash assumption of justification has been undermined. An old worry has returned—one that I thought I had sublimated many years ago. It is eating me up inside and as I stand here now, I am not sure I can live with it again. I cannot tolerate the possibility that what I did was wrong. Can you imagine living with the knowledge of what I have done? I can no longer imagine continuing to live. And so I say, let us pray:

Blue Star, We are Thy Tears, The Guidance of Gaia, We Seek;
Great Spirit, the Fire in our Eyes, Before Thee, We Speak.

Upon finishing these words, Zola Eblo gathers a pile of branches and throws them onto the fire. She stands there for a moment, letting the smoke wash over her in an act of purification. The flames are high and those closest to the pit are forced to shuffle backwards. But Zola stands there. Then, in a series of swift movements, she reaches into her pocket and douses herself with the accelerant she had used to ignite the fire earlier. Before anyone can react, Zola runs and throws herself into the centre of the fire.

With howls of anguish and distress, the people helplessly watch her burn. Someone rushes to tip over the barrels of drinking water in the hope of extinguishing the fire, but it is too little, too late. All that is achieved is to turn the bright bonfire into a smouldering source of thick smoke, which quickly encircles the stadium. Worse, the water rushes through the fire only to carry embers toward those sitting nearest the flames, causing people to stumble over each other as they try to avoid getting burnt.

Everywhere people are shouting in fear, anger, and confusion, and in the heat of the moment several men are seen fighting, for reasons that remain unclear. Desperately, Andrea Lorde moves to the front of the assembly in an attempt to re-establish some order, but her voice is lost completely in the commotion. In a panicked attempt to avoid the smoke, hundreds of people rush to the exits, creating a stampede that injures many. Chaos reigns for a time as the stadium clears. And then silence returns. Those few who chose to remain in the stadium, now almost empty, wait, in sacred community, for the sun to rise and the embers to die.

Together, alone, the last of the tribes slowly depart the dilapidated stadium and begin the journey back to their home regions. Nobody could have been satisfied with this conclusion to the gathering, but over the passing days, as the experience continues to wash over the tribespeople, most come to see that the abrupt finish to the ceremony ended up serving a philosophic purpose, leaving each individual and community to form their own conclusions in an uncertain moral universe.

What happened to Professor Senjen is now a matter of legend and lore. Some say he was lynched and hung from a tree as he tried to leave the stadium; others say he accepted the invitation to reside in Starfallen Grove; still others say he passed his final years in solitude planting trees in abandoned cities—whether out of guilt or hope, no one can be sure.

9 780648 840503